PRAISE FOR IRIS MORLAND

He Loves Me, He Loves Me Not

A hilarious, sexy and heartwarming romantic comedy...you do not want to miss this fun, feel-good romance.

— MARY DUBÉ, CONTEMPORARILY EVER AFTER

...refreshing, funny, emotionally charged, and very entertaining to read.

— CAROL, TIL THE LAST PAGE

There is humor, there is heart and there is heat in this story! I absolutely loved it! . . . Mari and Liam delivered. Yowza, their chemistry was palpable.

— BIBLIOPHILE CHLOE

Petal Plucker

Funny, charming, and utterly captivating! I devoured this sparkling read.

— ANNIKA MARTIN, NEW YORK TIMES BESTSELLING AUTHOR

Petal Plucker was funny, entertaining, fresh and fan-yourself-worthy . . . Their enemies-to-lovers romance is both charming, tender and steamy, and you'll love both of these characters (and their families!) and their sigh-worthy happily ever after.

— MARY DUBÉ, CONTEMPORARILY EVER AFTER

Morland has created a masterpiece of a romance . . . one of my favorite [books] of the year.

— CRISTIINA READS

Humorous, raunchy, and refreshing, Petal Plucker has rightfully earned its way, in my opinion, as one of the best romantic comedy [books] this year.

— CAROL, TIL THE LAST PAGE

MY ONE AND ONLY

This book was gripping, well written & the chemistry between the characters sizzled throughout this wonderful read.

— AMAZON REVIEW

ALL I WANT IS YOU

Another heartfelt, steamy, terrific story. This is an author who really knows how to create a story that catches a reader's attention and characters that capture her heart.

— BOOKADDICT

TAKING A CHANCE ON LOVE

Thea and Anthony are in for a surprise when it comes to the language of the heart . . . I am in awe.

— HOPELESS ROMANTIC BLOG

THEN CAME YOU

This story really pulled all my heartstrings. This was truly a beautiful story and makes you believe there really is true love out there.

— MEME CHANELL BOOK CORNER

ALSO BY IRIS MORLAND

HERON'S LANDING

Say You're Mine

All I Ask of You

Make Me Yours

Hold Me Close

THE FLOWER SHOP SISTERS

Oopsie Daisy

He Loves Me, He Loves Me Not

Petal Plucker

War of the Roses

LOVE EVERLASTING

including

THE YOUNGERS

Then Came You

Taking a Chance on Love

All I Want Is You

My One and Only

THE THORNTONS

The Nearness of You

The Very Thought of You

If I Can't Have You

Dream a Little Dream of Me

Someone to Watch Over Me

Till There Was You

I'll Be Home for Christmas

SAY YOU'RE MINE

HERON'S LANDING

IRIS MORLAND

BLUE VIOLET PRESS LLC

Say You're Mine (Heron's Landing Book 1)
Published by Blue Violet Press LLC
Seattle, Washington

Published 2020.

First edition published 2016 under the title Seduce Me Sweetly (Heron's Landing Book 1). Second edition 2020.

For my dad.

AUTHOR'S NOTE

Dear Readers,

Before you begin Adam and Joy's story, please know that *Say You're Mine* was previously published under the title *Seduce Me Sweetly*. This second edition has been lightly edited and changed to better fit the overall feel of the rest of my catalogue.

All my best,
    Iris

SAY YOU'RE MINE

CHAPTER ONE

Joy McGuire glanced down at her chipped manicure and sighed. She had a feeling this was going to be an omen for the rest of her week.

The movers weren't even close to arriving in Heron's Landing, and Joy had had to sleep on a few blankets and a jacket for a pillow the night prior. Her back aching and her neck sore, she could've cheerfully murdered someone when she'd gotten a call that the movers were lost—*again*—and they wouldn't be in town until later that evening.

It was nine o'clock AM. At least she'd driven with the majority of her clothes and toiletries, so she could put on clean underwear and wash her face. She just hoped she'd be able to sleep in a bed tonight, otherwise she was sorely tempted to book a room in the one inn this town of two hundred and fifty people hosted.

Heron's Landing was a far cry from Chicago: tiny and quintessentially Midwestern, it had a single main street with no more than a dozen shops and restaurants, while its main feature was a vineyard on the north side of town. Tourists wandered around, fanny packs and cameras in tow, taking photos of the old-timey architecture. It was the beginning of June, and the day would promise to be a fairly warm one. Cicadas hummed in the trees, and the trills of sparrows and wrens filled the air.

Sometimes Joy wondered if she'd completely lost her mind, moving here. But she'd wanted to start over, and what better way to start over than to move somewhere the complete opposite of what you were used to? Heron's Landing wasn't going to have the crime sprees and drug busts like Chicago would, but there were stories here. Joy was rather looking forward to writing pieces on the opening of a new restaurant or how the town came together to fix a senior citizen's roof. She wanted staid. Normal. Boring. She'd had enough drama to last a lifetime, thank you very much.

So, Heron's Landing it would be. At least for now. Glancing down at her chipped nail polish, Joy sincerely hoped there was at least one decent manicurist in the town. She really hated to have her nails go bare.

Wandering down main street, Joy found what she was looking for: a café. A café had coffee. And maybe some kind of pastry. Her stomach rumbled, and she realized she hadn't eaten since yesterday afternoon. She'd been so preoccupied with her lost movers that food had completely slipped her mind. Now her stomach was reminding her of her neglect, and she hoped this sleepy little café called Trudy's had more to it than just weak coffee and dry biscuits.

"Just one?" the hostess asked with a bright smile, and Joy nodded. The hostess—Grace, she read on her nametag—had her hair in a configuration of braids on top of her head, some falling down already. Her uniform had been haphazardly put on, and her skirt was crooked. Freckles dotted her peaches and cream complexion, and her smile could put any toothpaste commercial girl to shame. "Are you visiting?" Grace asked as she placed the menu in front of Joy. "Just so you know, our pancakes are kinda famous around here."

"No, I'm here to stay. At least for a little while." Joy glanced over the menu, but she was so tired that she could barely read the words in front of her.

Grace's eyebrows rose. "A new person? Oh, we haven't had a new person since…" She tapped her lip, thinking. "Well, probably not since I came back, but I'm not really *new*. Just one of the locals who couldn't stay away."

"Why'd you come back?" Joy couldn't help but ask. She'd grown up in Springfield, Illinois, but had been in Chicago for the last few years—but had never really felt particularly drawn to one place over the other.

"Oh well, I just graduated—a degree in studio art—and unfortunately for us artists, it's hard to make a living on painting and drawing." The brightness in Grace's smile turned brittle for a moment, like she hadn't wanted to return at all, and Joy felt a little guilty for pressing.

"I understand that all too well. I'm a writer. People are always trying to pay me in pats on the back."

"A writer! I don't know if we have any around here. Not beyond Mrs. Jenkins, who's always talking about writing that romance novel about Vikings. But she's been talking about that for twenty years now." Seeing the front door open, Grace added, "I have to get these guys, but Terry will take care of you. Welcome to town, Joy."

Joy ended up ordering the pancakes, and she couldn't help but agree with Grace: they were damn good. The coffee was strong and hot, and Joy slumped in the well-worn leather of the booth and simply enjoyed the food and drink. She hadn't really sat down in what felt like weeks: not with packing up her apartment in Chicago, driving five hundred miles south to Heron's Landing, trying to help her directionally-challenged movers get on the right highway, and then sleeping on the floor last night? It was a wonder she was still standing.

Having finished her pancakes, Joy wondered if she should go back to her apartment above Mike's general store—yes, a real general store, and Joy had fallen in love with it the moment she'd stepped inside it—but there was nothing there. She couldn't unpack; she couldn't set up her new bookshelves; she couldn't even cook something. She tapped her nails on the plastic tabletop, thinking. Maybe she could go for a walk? Explore the town? But at the thought, her body groaned. What she really wanted was to go take a nap, but that wasn't really a great idea, given her bed situation.

Beds inevitably made her think of her old apartment, overlooking Lake Michigan. Her bed was a brand-new, king-sized pillow-top with an expensive duvet and matching pillows. It had been a rather large splurge on her part—it wasn't as if she made a ton of money as a freelance journalist —but she'd always dreamed of a bed just like it. Even the bright white of the duvet hadn't put her off. Sure, it would be close to impossible to keep clean in the grand scheme of things, but what did she care? It was *hers*. And it was gorgeous.

Jeremy had made fun of her for it. *So I guess this means we aren't sleeping in the bed?* he'd said the moment he'd first seen it. Joy had shown him how wrong he'd actually been soon thereafter.

Joy bit her lip, covering how her body shivered when she thought of Jeremy. She'd left Chicago and her apartment and Lake Michigan and the trains and the bustle mostly because of him. She didn't want to admit that to herself, but it was true. The second she'd found out he'd been cheating on her with her supposed best friend Regina? Her world had fallen apart. She and Jeremy had been together for five years, and he repaid her by sleeping with the woman she'd loved as much as she'd loved Jeremy. The double betrayal had done a number on her, and because Joy preferred things to be clean and final, she'd cut off the both of them without looking back.

She wished cutting them out of her life had concluded everything. But the wound still gaped and bled, no matter how hard Joy tried to ignore it.

Shaking her head, she set some money on the table and got up, deciding that sitting and thinking about Jeremy wasn't going to improve her mood. She'd left Chicago for that very reason, and she refused to let his betrayal ruin this fresh start. As she made her way to the door, a man stepped in. He was tall—at least a head taller than Joy—with dark hair and dark eyes. But what brought her to attention the most was how rugged he was, with muscled forearms and a firm jaw sprinkled with stubble. He was also rather dirty, with leaves in his hair, and Joy found herself intrigued despite herself.

"When's the last time you took a bath? Did you roll in the mud this morning?" Grace demanded, her hands on her hips. She then looked at Joy, her expression changing to one of entreaty. "Let me get you a piece of cake to take home. We always give newcomers some."

The man made a face. "Since when was that a tradition?"

"Since this morning!" Grace called out from the kitchen.

Joy found herself standing next to the man, and she had to stop herself from staring at him. He wasn't handsome, per se, but he was striking, in a masculine kind of way. She'd gotten so used to men like Jeremy, who were always perfectly dressed and their hair perfectly coiffed, that she couldn't help but want to know more about a man who was the antithesis of the men she knew.

Or so she told herself when her heart wouldn't stop pounding. He was very tall, and very rugged, and his hands—

"I haven't seen you around here." The man held out his hand, surprisingly clean despite the rest of his appearance. "I'm Adam Danvers."

Joy had to tilt her head back to look at him. Damn, he was *tall*. She was of average height, and Jeremy had only been an inch or two taller than her. But this man seemed particularly giant. He took up the front entrance of the restaurant, his presence overwhelming. She could almost feel his body heat radiating, and her skin prickled.

She realized she was staring, and, embarrassed, finally extended her hand. "Joy McGuire. I've just moved to town."

Adam's eyebrows rose. "An actual new townsfolk? We haven't gotten one of those in a while. We get a lot of tourists, but not a lot of people staying here for good."

"Well, I like to be original."

Looking her up and down, Adam said, "I can see that."

Joy suddenly felt self-conscious: her long, purple hair and bright nails and arm tattoo hadn't been all that odd in Chicago. But here, she was like a cardinal amongst a bunch of plain, hardy sparrows. Well, not that Adam was even remotely like a sparrow. Joy thought he was more like a hawk: watchful, even cunning. There was something in his eyes that made both her heart pound and the storyteller in her want to know more about him. She'd had a few daydreams about finding some hot country guy out here as she drove the five hundred miles from Chicago, but she certainly hadn't thought she'd meet one on her first day.

"Here you go!" Grace handed Joy the piece of cake, now placed in a Styrofoam container. "It's fresh out of the oven this morning."

Joy knew she'd have to eat this soon, as she didn't have a fridge yet, but at Grace's happy smile, she didn't have the heart to tell her as much. "Thank you. I'm sure it's amazing."

"Oh, did you meet my brother? This is Adam. Adam, this is Joy. She's a writer."

Adam had stuffed his hands into his back pockets, and at Grace's words, he made a noise in the back of his throat. "A writer? What kind of writing?"

Joy cringed internally. She hated that question—it was almost impossible to talk about with people who weren't writers because it inevitably led to awkwardness—so she gave her standard answer: "I'm a freelance journalist, actually."

"A journalist? That's a first for this town." Adam's tone seemed, if not annoyed, at least not particularly enthused.

"I write primarily for online news blogs and magazines. Depends on what kind of stories come my way."

"So you wait for something bad to happen and then cash in on it."

"Adam!" Grace looked to Joy. "He's a bear in the morning without his coffee. Don't listen to him."

Joy, though, kept her gaze on Adam, refusing to be cowed. She'd gotten a variety of reactions to her profession over the years, but outright disdain was a rare one. She was torn

7

between outrage and curiosity: what would bring such a reaction from a guy she didn't even know? Had a journalist run over his dog or something? "No, I wait for something where the truth needs to be uncovered and brought to light," she explained, her voice edgy. If Joy was anything, she was not a woman easily intimidated. "Are you against telling the truth, Mr. Danvers?"

"If it hurts other people and it's only for your own gain, yes."

"Who's to say I do this only for monetary gain?"

Adam gestured, his mouth curling. "You do this to pay your bills. Sounds like you're getting something out of the deal."

Tipping her chin up, Joy crossed her arms. "And are you always this rude to people who have just moved here? Because if you're the welcome committee, it's a pretty shitty one."

"I'm not here to coddle anyone."

"Coddling is one thing. Being a jerk is another."

"I'm only saying what I think—"

Grace sighed, loudly. "Adam, will you shut up already? Here's your coffee—" she stuffed a cup into his hand, "—now get out. Go take a shower, too."

He looked at Grace, transferring his gaze away from Joy. Joy sighed inwardly, suddenly glad she wasn't the center of that angry look.

"And you, dear sister, need to learn that an iron is an invention that works." He pulled out a phone encased in pink and handed it to her. "Also, I came here to give you this. Mom texted me to tell me you left it at home again."

"Oh, I didn't even realize—thanks. But you're still a jerk." Grace play-kicked him, and Adam held up his hands.

"See you, Grace. See you around, Miss McGuire," he said in a tone that Joy knew wasn't at all trying to be polite.

As he stepped outside, she couldn't help but yell at his back, "It's Ms. McGuire because it's 2016, not 1916!" Turning back to Grace, Joy raised an eyebrow. "Your brother always this polite to strangers?"

Grace cringed. "Kind of. He's never been all that nice in general. Especially not since Carolyn died."

"Carolyn?"

"His wife. She died three years ago. She kept him from being outright mean, but now…" Sighing, the girl fiddled with her hair. "He's not been the same, you know?"

Joy did know. Or at least, she understood how heartbreak could mark a person. That didn't mean she would excuse his rudeness, but it at least offered somewhat of an explanation. "Just assure me he won't try to run me out of town for posting a story on the Internet."

"He can try, but I won't let him. Because you have to show me how you do your nails like that first."

Joy laughed. "Well, I've always paid someone else to do them for me, but I might have to figure it out on my own now. One of the sacrifices of small-town life, right?"

"Dana's the manicurist at the salon, and I think she could do something like that. Or at least near to it. But she just had a baby and is on maternity leave for a while, so I don't know when you could get an appointment with her."

Before Joy could rethink it, she said, "How about you come over to my place for a girl's night sometime this week? Once I get furniture, that is. I need some quality girl time. And we could even paint our nails."

"Oh, sure! I'd love to. I'll bring my famous Bloody Mary's."

"Sounds like a deal. I'll see you later, then?"

Grace called out her goodbye as Joy left the café, the sun so bright overhead that she had to shade her eyes.

What to do now? She could explore the town some more, but tiredness swamped her limbs at the thought. She desperately wanted to take a nap, but without a bed, that might be more pain than it was worth.

Cake in hand, Joy walked down Main Street, looking in shop windows as she passed. Eventually, she got to the outskirts of town and began walking a well-tread path that she thought would lead to the vineyard. The trees burst with color, emerald green in the sunlight, and she hadn't seen so much color in one place in what seemed like ages. Chicago was all grays and rust, metropolitan and metallic, but here, it seemed like technology hadn't even really touched it. They had apparently only recently gotten high-speed Internet, but otherwise, the area felt untouched. Virginal, almost. Joy smiled at the thought. The last place she thought she'd end up would be somewhere virginal in aspect, but her heart calmed simply being here.

If she ever thought this had been a poor decision, being in the midst of such natural beauty put those fears to rest.

Her phone rang, and looking at the number, she saw that it was from a Chicago line. Assuming it was the movers—were they lost a third time?—she picked up. "Hello?"

"Joy?"

She stilled, the voice on the other end one she'd recognize anywhere, but not one she ever wanted to hear again. "Why are you calling me?"

"Because you wouldn't pick up your phone or text me

back. Don't hang up on me. Please?" Her ex-friend Regina's voice was pleading. Almost like she was about to cry.

Torn between crying herself or telling Regina to go to hell, Joy said in a tight voice, "What do you want, then?"

"I wanted to make sure you were all right. You up and move to the middle of nowhere and we didn't know if you'd gotten there or if you were okay. Are you okay?"

Gritting her teeth, Joy continued to walk in a random direction, not even heeding the trees or the birds or the creek bed flowing next to her. Everything was eclipsed by Regina's voice, reminding her of everything she'd wanted to leave behind. "I'm fine. As fine as I can be after my boyfriend cheats on me with my best friend. So yeah, I'm great."

Regina sighed. "Look, I know I can't apologize enough—"

"No, you can't."

"But that doesn't mean I don't still care about you. Jeremy, too. We want you to be happy."

Joy laughed, a bitter laugh. Regina wanted her to be happy, after she'd destroyed her life? "You have a lot of nerve. I'm not remotely interested in your condescending hopes that I be happy. You know what would've made me happy? My best friend not sleeping with my boyfriend." She knew the words were harsh, cruel. But she hadn't spoken to Regina since she'd found out about the affair, and they came spilling out, like a dam breaking. "So spare me your attempts at reconciliation."

Silence on the other end. Then, "Fine. I won't try to contact you again."

"Please don't."

"Bye, Joy."

Joy felt nothing as she turned around, walked back to Main Street. She felt nothing as she climbed the stairs to her apartment, as she set the already melted cake on the kitchen ledge. She felt nothing as she kicked off her shoes and as she climbed into her pile of blankets on the floor.

But the nothingness then filled with something: it cracked, the wound gushing blood once again, and tears flowed in a torrent that she couldn't stop even if she wanted to.

CHAPTER TWO

Walking the rows of his family's vineyard, River's Bend, Adam felt the world on his shoulders. He passed between the rows, the sun beating down overhead. Where had this warmth and dryness been when they'd needed it? Now, though, it was too late: the amount of buds that should've been on the vines was fewer even than last year. Fewer buds meant fewer grapes, and without grapes, little wine could result.

Adam wiped his brow. The humidity was creeping up already, despite it being early morning. It would probably reach close to one hundred degrees, as was common in the middle of June. Mosquitoes buzzed about, but he hardly noticed them. He probably should've doused himself in bug spray before coming out, but what were a few mosquito bites? He was used to them by now. Any Missouri country boy was used to bugs biting and buzzing and flying about.

At any rate, the bugs weren't the problem. His sad grape crop was—the extensive rains of March and April had devastated the vines, causing a lot of the new buds to fall off and mildew to wreck havoc on the rest of the crop. What resulted was a sad amount of buds now that would change into hard, green grapes before veraison, or ripening, began in mid-August. If this had only happened this year, it would've been difficult, but not impossible. But last year had been a drought, and the year before that had been rainy, and this year had been particularly brutal with all of the rain. The river that flowed just east of Heron's Landing had almost flooded the town; Adam and his family had had sandbags on hand just in case.

Adam's head hurt. He didn't know what to do now. He knew already that the crop would be dismal, and that the vineyard had been hurting for some time. The recession plus climate change had hurt farmers all over the state.

Bending down, he fingered the little buds that had managed to survive the spring. These Norton grapes would eventually become a full-bodied, berry-rich red wine, one of River's Bend's signature bottles. People from all over the country—even from across oceans—had visited their vineyard to taste their wines. Adam could remember as a child how he'd looked up to his father, watching him run River's Bend with precision and insight, taking it to new heights that his grandfather couldn't even have imagined.

Now Adam was its owner and manager, and his laurels included three years of bad crop and a business that was sinking as surely as a rock thrown into the river. He couldn't exactly control the weather, but that didn't help his pride one bit. "I was supposed to be even better than my dad and grand-dad," he told the buds, which bounced slightly in the morning breeze. "And now look at me: wondering if I can even keep the entire thing open for next year."

He made his way back to the main building of River's Bend, which included a renowned restaurant and held wine tastings every weekday. He entered the back entrance, making his way to his office without being seen by either his secretary Kerry O'Brian or his executive chef Jaime Martínez. He didn't really want to talk about anything at the moment: he preferred to think in peace, figure out solutions to his problems without running to anyone else.

But as luck would have it, Jaime was already there, waiting for him. The man knew Adam way too well, and Adam was tempted to tell his chef and friend to get the hell out. Jaime was striking—that was what Grace had called him, and Adam had to agree, at least inwardly—with dark eyes and medium-brown skin, his hair similarly dark. His parents had immigrated to the States from El Salvador; Jaime had been born shortly after their arrival.

"Already have the menu ready for today?" Adam asked Jaime casually, sitting down at his desk.

"You act like I don't know this winery as well as you do. And yeah, it's ready, and my new sous chef is getting everything prepared while I talk to the boss." Jaime sat down in the chair opposite Adam, propping his feet on the desk.

Adam raised an eyebrow. "A new sous chef? I thought you already hired a new sous chef. Or did he quit after you made him cry?"

"I don't make them cry; they just realize they aren't up to my standards. Not my fault they're graduating these losers without even knowing how to butcher an entire cow."

Adam had a feeling a lot of chefs wouldn't know what to do with a whole cow, but Jaime had exacting standards. Jaime was an extremely hard worker, and he'd transformed the restaurant the moment he'd arrived. Adam couldn't fault him for riding his sous chefs as well.

"So are you here to tell me your newest sous chef is threatening to sue because you're mean, or do you have something else to tell me?" Adam asked.

"Are you always this pleasant in the morning?"

"Maybe if you'd brought me some coffee before you decided to invade my office, I might be," Adam replied wryly.

Jaime gave him the bird, but it was done with a smile. "I'm not your kitchen boy, asshole. And I wanted to talk to you about opening up the vineyard for events. Again. You said if the crop was as bad as last year you'd consider it. Or did you conveniently forget that?"

Turning away, Adam turned on his computer, gazing at his vague reflection in the glass of the monitor. Yes, he'd remembered; no, he didn't want to consider it. It seemed straightforward, he knew—the vineyard needed the business, business meant money, ergo, they should do it—but Jaime didn't understand that it would change the heartbeat of the vineyard as well. Not to mention, they'd tried doing events a few years ago, and it'd been a disaster all around. Adam shuddered, remembering how the bride had yelled at him, accusing him of ruining her special day.

River's Bend had always prided itself on not becoming more of an event spot than a vineyard—no brides crying about it being too hot outside, no grooms too drunk to make it down the aisle—and Adam hadn't seen a reason to change things then and didn't see a reason to change things now. His granddad and dad hadn't done weddings and such, so why should he?

Remembering how they'd tried to expand the vineyard into events last go-around made anxiety congeal in his stomach. Four years ago, River's Bend had needed more revenue, and Adam's father Carl had still been the de facto manager, with Adam handling much of the accounting and bookkeeping. Carl had decided to try out a few events one summer, telling Adam that the two of them together could more than handle brides getting down the aisle and keeping the grooms from falling into the river.

"You know how much money people spend on weddings these days?" Carl had said. "If we could just get a tiny slice of that, we'd get this place out of the red."

Adam hadn't been sure—what did they know about event planning beyond a few wine-tasting classes? Plus, they hardly had time to run the vineyard as it was, let alone weddings. But he'd agreed, hoping that he was just being a butthead—as Grace liked to call him—and that it would turn out to be a great revenue generator.

Unsurprisingly to most everyone except Carl, it had failed. Spectacularly.

Carl didn't know how to deal with nervous, emotional brides, and his strong suit wasn't organization or event planning. When the big day arrived, nothing was planned like how the bride had wanted: the chairs were wrong, the aisle runner was wrong, the gazebo was wrong. They'd even made a chocolate cake instead of a red velvet one. It'd had been so disastrous that the bride had burst into tears at her own reception, and had promptly told everyone she knew to never, ever get married at River's Bend.

"Yeah, I remember," Adam eventually replied. "You have some grand plan to make that work this time around, or are you just shooting the breeze again? You remember what happened last time. It was a complete disaster, and it lost us money at the end of the day."

Sighing, Jaime set his feet down onto the floor. "Yeah, I remember. But, look, you know as well as I do that we aren't going to recoup our losses from last year. We were hit hard by the drought last summer, and now with all of the rain from this spring, the crop is going to be poor. You know it, I know it, everyone and their mom down in town knows it. So we have to find a solution that brings in money. Just because we failed once, doesn't mean we fail a second time. Make sense?"

"Sure it does. But who's going to handle all of these events? You? Me?" He scoffed. "Last time it was me, and we know how well that worked. Do I really look like the type of person who wants to talk to demanding brides-to-be, or even worse, their mothers?"

"I'm not saying it would be easy. But there has always been interest in this place hosting events, and it would be a waste to continue to turn away that business just because it wouldn't be your favorite thing. Plus, most people have forgotten about Becky Harris's infamous Yelp review."

Part of Adam had to agree, although he didn't want to. But even if they started to do weddings here again, they didn't have the money to hire someone, anyway. "It's not just that it wouldn't be my 'favorite thing.' I know nothing about event planning. Kerry is already beyond capacity handling restaurant reservations and the wine tastings all week long. Would you add wedding coordination on top of that?"

Jaime made a sound of frustration. "Will you at least consider it?"

"Sure. But that's not going to change the fact that we have no money to do it."

The truth was that they could probably finagle a way to hire a new person—at least part-time—but Adam wasn't going to change River's Bend like this without a fight. He hadn't fought hard enough last time, and it'd been a disaster. And even if they did hire someone, who was to say it'd be successful? Then they'd really be in trouble.

Wanting to change the subject, Adam asked, "What's on the menu for today?"

"Roasted catfish with sweet corn hash on a bed of arugula with the Sauvignon Blanc to accompany it."

Smiling, Adam couldn't help but comment, "To think when you started you thought catfish wasn't worth feeding to a feral cat."

"It's edible when I cook with it." Standing, Jaime eyed Adam for a second. "I know you won't throw away a good opportunity without consideration. Right?"

Adam's phone rang, and seeing that it was Kerry, he said, "I gotta take this. But I will consider what you're saying, okay? You haven't led me in the wrong direction yet."

Jaime nodded and left Adam to pick up the phone.

"Kerry?"

"Mr. Danvers, we have a visitor who'd like a tour today, if you have time."

Adam glanced at the clock, and then back at his computer. Technically, he didn't have the time, but did he really want to be shut up in his office when he could be talking about River's Bend to someone who was interested in the place?

He didn't have to give tours—they had other staff who did —but if he could manage it, Adam preferred to be the one who did it. Mostly because he loved showing the place off to people. It was his family's legacy, and pride filled him each time he explained how they grew the grapes, what was involved in harvesting them, and what types of wine they made. He wasn't necessarily a chatty man by nature, but give him a subject he enjoyed, and he wouldn't stop talking about it. Grace liked to tease him about it, but Adam didn't really mind. He did love talking about River's Bend, and why shouldn't he? It was a true jewel here in the heart of Missouri.

Standing up, he snagged his phone and sunglasses as he headed to the front desk. His mom would probably frown at him for not putting on sunscreen, but he was tan enough that he wouldn't get burned after a few hours in the sun. He wondered who had come to the vineyard today, and a person alone? That was interesting. Usually it was couples or families who wanted tours, but occasionally a lone man or woman would show up, too.

As he stepped into the area where the front desk was located, he heard a voice that seemed familiar. He stopped, listened, and then as he rounded the corner, he realized exactly who it was: Joy McGuire, journalist and newcomer who he'd...*spoken to* at Trudy's.

Seeing her now, he couldn't help but marvel at how colorful she was: purple hair with a top that showed a hint of midriff and tiny shorts hugging her ass and hips. She raised her eyebrows when she noticed him, and he had to bite back a groan. He really didn't want to deal with this right now, and he especially didn't want to deal with how he traced the lines of her body and wished her top edged higher so he could see more of her creamy skin.

"Oh, Mr. Danvers! Glad you're here. Have you met Joy? She just moved here," Kerry said.

Looking straight at Joy, Adam said without a hint of irony, "Yeah, we've met."

CHAPTER THREE

Joy had needed a project. She had a few clients she still wrote for long-distance, but she wanted to sink her teeth into something here in Heron's Landing. That was why she'd come, wasn't it? To get to know a new town and new people? The town wasn't hustling and moving as quickly as Chicago. In fact, it moved about quickly as an elderly turtle swimming through mud. But that didn't stop her from looking around for stories.

Drumming her fingers on the arm of her couch—the movers had finally arrived that morning—Joy brainstormed for a few hours. Perhaps she could interview the owner of Trudy's? Or maybe Mike in the general store downstairs had something worth writing about? She pursed her lips, thinking.

Of course, there was always the vineyard, River's Bend. It was the jewel of Heron's Landing, but that seemed cliché. Plus, it was five miles from her apartment, and she really didn't want to drive that gravel road to get out there. The day had already edged into one-hundred-degree territory:

thinking about tromping around the vineyard with the sun beating down did not sound remotely pleasant.

But after an hour or two, Joy realized she'd be remiss in ignoring the vineyard right off the bat. It would be a great introduction to Heron's Landing. Nibbling on her pen, she reconsidered. Before she closed her laptop, she grabbed her handy notepad, and then made her way to her car to drive those five miles. What else did she have to do? Think about what she'd left behind in Chicago?

She shuddered at the thought. River's Bend it was.

When she walked up to the front desk in the vineyard's main building, Joy had to admit she was impressed: the room was decorated with modern furniture, with cream couches and chairs surrounding simple wooden coffee tables. Wildflowers in vases dotted the tables, and to her relief, no dead animals hung from the walls. River's Bend may have been in the country, but it didn't scream country, either.

"How can I help you?" the front desk clerk asked. She was young, perhaps mid-twenties, with a full face and startling white teeth. Pretty in a milkmaid kind of way. Joy could just imagine her cheeks flushed, carrying a pail from the barn in the early morning hours.

Thrusting out her hand, Joy said, "I'm Joy McGuire. I recently moved here from Chicago, and I thought I'd get a tour around this place. I've heard so much about it already."

The girl shook her hand vigorously. "Miss McGuire! Yes, I heard we had a newcomer. I'm Kerry." She pointed to her engraved name badge. "Let me see if Mr. Danvers is available for a tour. He likes to do them himself, as the owner."

Alarm bells rung in Joy's head at the name. *Danvers? Not*

the *Mr. Adam Danvers, who'd so courteously welcomed her here? He was the owner of River's Bend?*

"I'm sure he's much too busy," Joy said with a wave. "Could you show me around instead?"

"Oh, you would much rather have Mr. Danvers. He knows *everything* about this place." Kerry picked up her phone, expertly dialing an extension. She smiled up at Joy before saying into the phone, "Mr. Danvers, we have a visitor who'd like a tour today, if you have time. Yes, mmhmm. Okay. Thank you." Hanging up, she said to Joy, "He'll be right up. Would you like something to drink while you wait?"

Joy shook her head. Only in a small town like this would the owner himself take some random on a tour. And only in a small town like this would the owner be the guy who had insulted her only the day before. She sighed inwardly. That was just her luck, always. Couldn't she catch a break? And how could she very well do a story on this place when Mr. Journalists-Are-Satan's-Spawn was the owner?

He'd probably kick her out on her ass the second he saw her.

When he finally arrived, Joy's heart sped up just at the sight of him, because she was an idiot who made poor decisions. God, he was handsome, in an asshole kind of way. Dark hair, dark eyes—which were her weakness, even though Jeremy had been the opposite in coloring—and his jeans slung low on his hips. She bit the inside of her cheek, trying to keep the stem of laughter from bubbling out. She tended to giggle when she was uncomfortable, and by God, the thought of wandering around with Adam Danvers for an hour or two made her painfully uncomfortable. For more than one reason, too.

"Oh, Mr. Danvers! Glad you're here. Have you met Joy? She just moved here," Kerry said.

He looked straight at Joy. His voice was gruff as he said, "Yeah, we've met."

Ha, he sure had that right! They'd met and he'd been a dick of the highest order to her for no damn reason. The childish part of her wanted to stomp on his instep and watch him cry, while the other wished she'd worn a nicer bra and put on more mascara.

Stop being stupid and vain, her brain admonished. *Do you really want to get into Mr. Asshole's pants? The pants would probably yell at you for being nosy.*

Joy, though, wasn't one to be cowed—especially not by jerk men. Instead, she preferred to needle and rile them until they begged her to stop (okay, that had only happened once, but she enjoyed the thought). She may be girly and had purple hair and loved kittens and cried at episodes of *Undercover Boss,* but she wasn't a wimp, either.

She shot her hand out. "We have met. How are you today, Mr. Danvers?"

He took her hand with an eyebrow quirk. "Fine," he replied. "You?"

"Oh, I'm fantastic. I thought I'd do a story on this place. You know, a story written by a *journalist.* That kind of story?"

Oblivious to the undercurrent, Kerry exclaimed, "That's a great idea! I didn't know you were a writer, Miss McGuire."

"Call me Joy. And yes, I am. I'm a very unprincipled, naughty journalist." She batted her eyelashes at Adam, waiting for him to call her bluff.

Instead, he said nothing for a moment before he turned to

Kerry. "We'll be gone for an hour. Call me on my cell if something comes up."

"Sounds good. Have fun you two." Kerry winked and sat back down at her desk, humming merrily as she typed something.

"Ready?" Adam eyed her, liked he was expecting her to renege.

Ha! Fat chance. "Ready when you are," she said sweetly.

Making their way outside, she wished she'd put on sunscreen before she'd left. She shaded her eyes against the bright, summer sun. Maybe she'd be okay? It shouldn't take that long. But then she looked at her pale arms and sighed inwardly. Hopefully Adam the Grump talked quickly and she'd avoid turning into a lobster.

As it turned out, he didn't talk quickly, but he did walk quickly. She had to almost jog to keep up with his long-legged strides. Why did tall people always do this? Couldn't they slow down for their shorter peers without losing stock in the tall people's club? Joy huffed behind him; he glanced back at her but said nothing.

I hope you walk so fast you fall in a ditch, she thought, slapping at a mosquito. *Asshole.*

Once they arrived at the vineyard itself, he stopped, hands in his pockets. He seemed to be taking in the scenery, and she had to admit it was beautiful: River's Bend sat on bluffs overlooking the river, and the trees were emerald green with summer foliage. The vines themselves didn't look like they had much on them yet, but she knew nothing about running a vineyard or how to grow grapes.

Eventually, Adam said gruffly, "I guess I'll start with my granddad buying this piece of land."

He seemed...uncomfortable. Like he'd never done this before, which was odd, considering he was the owner and Kerry had mentioned he often did the tours. Shrugging inwardly, Joy pulled out her notebook to scribble down quotes and any useful information she could use writing the piece. He may not like journalists—or her being one—but that wasn't going to stop her from writing what she wanted. First Amendment and all that.

He glanced at her as she wrote down things, explaining the history of River's Bend and how the vineyard was started. Seventy years ago, Thaddeus Danvers had purchased this land for a dime an acre, and soon discovered it would be an ideal place for a vineyard. His first crops hadn't yielded much in the way of drinkable wine, but after trying various types of grapes, he ended up making the first batch of red wine that was sold at the World's Fair.

"Soon, River's Bend was attracting all kinds of people, including the governor of Missouri at the time. Most people don't think of the Midwest as ideal wine-making country, but the climate actually works fairly well for grape crops. Soon after River's Bend, other vineyards were started across the state."

Joy took notes, nodding every so often. They'd wandered down the paths through the vines, and she didn't even realize he'd stopped talking until she heard him clear his throat.

"Can I ask what you're taking notes for?"

She stopped. Looked up. Did he really need to ask? "I want to do a story about this place," she explained. "And usually when you interview someone, you take notes."

Adam grimaced at the word "story," like she'd just told him she was planning on peeing on his plants in front of guests.

"I'm sure that's all well and good, but River's Bend doesn't need a story written about it."

"Why do you say that like I'm going to write a *National Inquirer*-esque story, like 'Vineyard Owner Keeps Twenty Secret Wives in the Basement!' or something? You realize not all journalists are creeps, right?"

"Not in my experience."

Okay, now he was just being a dick. Again. Stuffing her notepad into her shorts pocket, Joy crossed her arms, tapping her foot against the dark soil. "So I'm a creep? Is that what you think after knowing me for less than a day and having a grand total of thirty-minutes worth of conversation with me?"

His eyes widened, like he was surprised she'd fight back. Well, maybe the women in Heron's Landing didn't, but Joy McGuire never backed down from a fight. It was one of her better qualities, she thought.

"Look, I own and run this place. I realize I can't stop you from writing what you want, but I'd ask you not to write a story about River's Bend," he said.

"Sure, but only if you tell me why."

That got a reaction. It was still subtle—the man didn't seem like he was capable of gobs of intense emotion—but she still noticed it. It was a little tick in his jaw, and a narrowing of the eyes. It made him look dark and brooding, and even though she still wanted to stomp on his foot, she also found herself intrigued despite herself.

"I don't have to explain myself to you," he replied in clipped tones. "Now, do you want to finish this tour, or should we head back?"

Joy almost pulled her notepad out just to spite him, but based on his thunderous expression, she decided not to push her luck. He could very well throw her over his shoulder and carry her to his lair for that kind of a stunt. Which, really, sounded kind of amazing for a story.

"Show me the way, sir," she said with a flourish. He snorted, but continued on.

As Adam talked about winemaking and the grapes and even the fertilizer, she had to admit that she wasn't the least bit bored. The man seemed to come alive as he talked: it was that alone that kept her listening. She'd never been the type of person to listen to someone talk for a long stretch of time—she had the attention span of a squirrel most days—but as she followed Adam along, she drank in every word.

It almost helped that the man himself was attractive. She wouldn't deny it: he was handsome, and if he weren't a dick, she'd climb him like a tree. She hadn't gotten laid in months—not since Jeremy dumped her—and her libido had been whining to her for a while. But her heart remained sore and the cracks hadn't healed yet, and she'd been determined to keep her pants on to avoid any more heartbreak. She'd never been good about separating sex and love, and the last thing she needed right now was more pain and anguish when it came to a man.

Joy was still a writer, though, and she always enjoyed watching people. She watched as Adam bent down and showed her the little buds that would somehow turn into grapes come August. His dark hair tended to get in his eyes, and he brushed it away without even noticing it. His hands were tan, the fingers long and the nails well groomed, and she noticed that he still wore a wedding band. Grace had told her he'd lost his wife, and at the memory, she felt a sudden surge of sympathy for him.

He was too young to lose a spouse; they couldn't have been married for long. She watched him as he rose, seemingly unaware of where her mind had gone. She wondered how he'd met his wife, if they'd wanted to have kids, if he ever thought he'd marry again.

And then she shook her head, as it wasn't any of her business anyway. She had a tendency to be rather nosy—came with the territory of being a writer—and if given a morsel of a good story, she wanted to follow it to the bitter end like a bloodhound. But this wasn't a good story: it was Adam's life.

"Your shoulders are all red," he pointed out abruptly. "Probably should've put on sunscreen."

Okay, it was his life, but he was still a dick. She looked at her shoulders—shit, he was right. She was sunburned.

"I hate you, sun!" she said with fist raised.

Adam looked beyond into the vineyard, and then started back to the main building without explanation.

"Hey, are we done? You didn't even show me those vines over there." She hurried to catch up.

"The tour doesn't include the entire vineyard. And I have work to do."

Joy scrunched her nose at his back. "'I have work to do,'" she muttered under her breath. "Probably working on pulling that stick out of his ass."

If he heard her, he made no sign of it. She sighed, feeling the sting of her sunburn already. Chicago wasn't really a place to get a tan, so she should've known better than to go outside in full-sun for more than five seconds. She could hear her mom's voice in her head, admonishing her. *You'll get skin cancer doing that! Remember Aunt Marta and her moles that spread all over her back?*

How could she forget Aunt Marta's moles? She shuddered.

She wondered if Adam had any moles on his back. Probably not. He seemed like he'd never allow himself something so human. And then that thought inevitably led to what he'd look like without his shirt, and how muscular his back—and front—would be. Would he have hair on his chest, or did he do a little waxing down here in the boonies? She imagined he'd have a bit of a happy trail, leading down to the ultimate prize—

Whoa, do not go there, she told herself sternly. *You cannot, will not, under any circumstances, get it on with this asshole.* Her mind was stern, but her libido kept up the whining, anyway. Couldn't she just have a tiny, measly little fling? Just a grab and go without getting all entangled?

As Adam opened the door for her, his gaze on her face, she knew the answer to that: nope, she'd probably fall for him and end up begging him to marry her. Mostly because she was the queen of poor decisions in regard to men. Look at Jeremy: she'd known he was questionable from the start, but she'd thought she could fix him. Love him enough to transform him, like Jane Eyre did for Rochester. Beauty and the Beast and true love conquers all. But then Jeremy had boned her best friend and said he'd gotten bored with her—his fiancée! —and now look where she was: twenty-nine, single, and lusting after a guy who'd insulted her multiple times.

"Did you have a good time?" Kerry asked brightly before gasping. "Oh no, you got sunburned!"

Was everyone in town going to point this out to her? Joy had to bite her tongue to avoid saying something snarky. "Yeah, looks like it. I'm used to it by now." She shrugged.

"It looks pretty bad, though. I hope it doesn't blister."

Joy looked at her shoulders: definitely red, but not as red as that one time at band camp that had resulted in a patch of blisters all over her shoulders. That had been a real treat.

"Well, I better get going," she began, but that was when Adam held up a hand.

"Wait here just a second." Before Joy could respond—was he bringing her a souvenir bottle of wine?—he walked off into what she assumed were the vineyard's offices.

"He sure is a peach," she said with an eye roll. "How do you put up with him?"

Kerry smiled. "I know he doesn't have the best manners, but he's a good man. Works really hard on this place. And I know he's been concerned about keeping it going, lately."

That was interesting news, and the nosy bloodhound in Joy perked up immediately. Was the vineyard hurting? Maybe even closing? Was that why Adam had the manners of a caveman?

But before she could interrogate the innocent front desk girl, Adam returned with a green bottle in hand. "Here," he said gruffly. "This will help with the burn."

Taking it, Joy realized it was aloe vera. He'd brought her this out of...kindness? Thoughtfulness? She was so shocked she couldn't speak. She stared at the plastic bottle filled with green goo and then looked up at Adam.

He seemed suddenly discomfited, and he shifted on his heels.

"Thank you," she finally responded. "This will help a lot."

Joy could feel Kerry staring at them. The girl had probably never seen her boss be blatantly helpful to anyone before.

"You're welcome," he said.

The moment stretched until it was awkward, so Joy did

what she always did: made it more awkward by giggling. She giggled like a girl, hand over her mouth. And then, when she saw Adam's face—surprised, bemused, annoyed?—she grabbed her purse and skittered out of there, choking on her laughter all the way home.

CHAPTER FOUR

"It's so nice of you to join us," Julia Danvers said as she kissed Adam's cheek. "We haven't seen you in ages."

They'd actually seen him...well, two weeks ago? Three? Adam couldn't remember, and guilt coiled in his gut. His parents only lived a few miles from his own house, but sometimes it felt like they lived on the other side of the country when he got swamped with working at River's Bend. And his mom was extremely talented at letting him know when he'd stayed away for too long.

"He just didn't feel like eating another Hot Pocket for dinner," Grace said. She laughed at her brother's expression. "You know I'm right—you eat the same as an eighteen-year-old freshman in college."

"Can it, Squirt," Adam growled. "Or I'm going to tell Mom and Dad about the Merlot Incident of 2013."

Grace blushed bright red.

"What Merlot Incident? What in the world are you talking about?" Carl Danvers asked as he entered the dining room, slapping a newspaper against his thigh. The patriarch of the

Danvers family was still a good-looking man in his mid-sixties, with salt and pepper hair and a neatly trimmed beard that tended to frame a perpetual frown. He wasn't an unhappy man, but instead tended toward seriousness; people who didn't know him well assumed he wasn't the nicest person, but they were unaware of how dedicated he was to both his family and his community.

"Oh nothing, Dad. Adam's just talking shit again," Grace said before she stuck her tongue out at her brother.

"No swearing at the table. I'm going to start a swear jar if you keep that up, young lady." Carl opened his newspaper with a flourish.

Adam laughed into his fist while Grace shot daggers at him.

"Goodness, aren't you two too old to squabble?" Julia set a bowl of mashed potatoes on the table in front of Adam, but she slapped his hand away when he was about to serve himself. "You two act like a bunch of kindergarteners."

"It's not my fault Adam has the maturity of a five year old," Grace said with an eyelash flutter. "How quickly did you insult Ms. McGuire after being introduced? Five seconds? One?"

Adam felt an uncustomary flush crawl up his face at the memory: he had been unaccountably rude to Joy, even if his reasons made sense to him. And at the thought of Joy, he remembered her laughter as she'd left River's Bend, when he'd so stupidly given her that bottle of aloe vera. He thought about how she'd listened to him explain the ins and outs of the vineyard. How she'd taken notes with her ridiculous pink pen, and how she'd seemed like this exotic, colorful bird in the midst of drab sparrows.

God, now he was going to start writing poetry about her? He tipped back his bottle of beer at the thought.

"Who's Ms. McGuire?" Carl asked, behind his paper.

Julia snatched the paper from him when she'd set the last plate of food on the table. "No reading at the table. And she's the new woman come to town, right?"

Grace nodded. "She came here from Chicago. She's a writer."

"Oh, how nice," Julia said, sitting down. "Adam, will you do grace?"

Grace made a face at him. He closed his eyes and dreamed about pushing his sister's face into the mashed potatoes as he thanked the Lord for the food before them.

The conversation flowed around the usual topics: the vineyard, the news in town, Grace's painting, and eventually flowed back to the topic of Joy McGuire. Heron's Landing received so few newcomers—people unrelated to anyone else in the town—that whenever it did happen, that person became the topic of conversation for at least a month. Adam assumed it was a town rule at this point.

"What brings a writer from Chicago to this place?" Carl asked as he cut up his steak. "Seems like the last place someone like that would move."

Grace said, "Maybe she needed a change of pace? Some place to detox?"

Carl grunted.

"I think it's lovely," Julia said, smiling at her family. With her light blonde hair and with only a few wrinkles on her face, Julia seemed years younger than fifty-nine. But she'd always prided herself on a neat, put-together appearance, and even when sitting with her family for dinner, she wore a pearl necklace and her hair up in a tidy bun. Adam hadn't seen his mom wear something like sweatpants in all the years he'd known her, although she'd traded in her heels for flats now that she was older. "When can I meet this young woman?" Julia asked. "Where is she staying?"

"Above the general store," Grace responded. "She has the apartment up there."

Julia said, "I assume she's unmarried?"

Joy's ring-less left hand flashed in Adam's mind, and he was annoyed at himself for looking in the first place. What did it matter to him whether or not Joy McGuire was married? It wasn't as if they could date.

At the thought of dating Joy—kissing Joy, touching Joy— Adam's body turned hot, and he finished off his beer to help stem the tide of whatever it was he was feeling right now.

"No, she's not married. But I think she may have left someone behind in Chicago," Grace said. "When she comes to Trudy's in the morning, sometimes I watch her, and she seems...sad."

Carl glanced at his youngest, his eyebrows lowered. "And what did I tell you about speculating about people?"

"That everyone does it, I just happen to say it out loud?" Grace said with a bright smile.

"Dad's right," Adam said suddenly. He didn't want to talk about Joy anymore, and he especially didn't want to talk about her unmarried state, either. "It's none of our business."

Grace protested, but Julia gave her The Look. Grace quieted, but not without a glare at Adam for getting her in trouble in the first place.

"Speaking of business, how is the old place doing?" Carl asked. "The buds looking good?"

If Adam didn't want to talk about Joy, he sure as hell didn't want to talk about River's Bend. But at his dad's expectant expression, he replied, "The ones that survived all of that rain look good. But it looks like this harvest won't be a great one." He sawed into his steak, not wanting to see his dad's face. What must he think of his oldest son, who'd had three years in a row of bad harvest? The disappointment of his dad was one of the top three things Adam never wanted to experience, and now it was happening—again.

"Well, you can't control the weather, Adam," Julia said prosaically. "Remember '83, Carl? That was one of the worst harvests we ever had. But we bounced back, just like you will." She patted Adam's hand like he was little boy, but hearing his mom's encouragement bolstered his own mood somewhat.

"Jaime says that you might start doing events again." Grace's voice was cool, offhand, but she knew she was throwing a bomb onto the table.

Adam glared at her with an expression saying, *I'll get you for this later.*

"Events?" Carl set down his fork and knife. "Son, you know what happened the last time."

Adam said, "Of course I do. And we've only discussed it—we've made no decision otherwise."

"I think it's a great idea," Grace offered. "You could hire someone part-time to be an events coordinator." She gasped, her silverware clattering to her plate. "You know who you should hire? Ms. McGuire! She could do marketing and social media. Even write up stories about the events you're doing—"

"Absolutely not." Adam knew his voice was too harsh, but he couldn't listen to Grace prattle on about things she didn't remotely understand. He saw his sister bite her lip, her expression hurt and annoyed, but he couldn't be sorry for that. "If we end up doing events—which is unlikely—we'll be doing it without some flashy journalist turning River's Bend into a wedding hub instead of a vineyard."

The table fell silent. They all remembered what had happened the last time, but they also knew that Adam could be as stubborn as the best of them, too. Just because they failed once, didn't necessarily mean they'd fail again. But Grace was staring at her plate morosely, and Carl never chose to enter family fights unless absolutely forced to.

The family mediator, Julia finally said, "Let us know how we can help. I know you're hesitant to change things, Adam, but you're smart enough to know when to change course, too."

Adam did know that. Deep down inside, he had a feeling they'd have to expand the vineyard into doing events, but he wanted to avoid that for as long as possible. Like he'd told Jaime, he didn't really have the money for a full-time event coordinator—possibly a part-time one, but that was it—and even then, that didn't mean success.

"How is Jaime, by the way?" Julia asked. Her glance landed on Grace, who looked up from her plate with a slight blush.

"How should I know?" Grace said. "I barely see him."

Everyone in the family—and probably the entire town— knew that Grace Danvers had nursed a crush on Jaime Martínez since he'd arrived in Heron's Landing. But Jaime was seven years her senior, and her brother was his boss, so any interaction had been strictly platonic. This was fine with Adam: his baby sister was too young to date, and although Jaime was a great guy, he had a feeling the two of them were too different to rub along well. Plus, Jaime was his employee, so that made things extra awkward.

"He's great," Adam offered, giving his sister a reprieve. "Although if he keeps firing sous chefs, I'm going to kick his ass."

"Language," Carl said.

"We should invite him to dinner more often. I can't imagine he enjoys eating alone. Don't you think, dear?" Julia said as she turned to her husband.

Since Carl now lived with two women exclusively, Adam had a feeling his dad would love to live in a bachelor pad every once in a while. But his dad was smart enough to say, "Sure, invite him."

"He'll take Gavin's place," Grace said. Gavin Danvers was the second-oldest brother, but he'd moved away from Heron's Landing years ago and rarely visited anymore. Adam had spoken to him maybe a month ago, but Gavin had never been particularly chatty to begin with. And now that he was having issues in his marriage again, he was more taciturn. Downright surly, really. He and his wife Teagan had been having trouble for a while now, mostly due to Teagan's battle with her mental health. They also had a young daughter, Emma, who the family had only gotten to see a handful of times.

Julia sighed sadly at the name of her other son, but no one else felt compelled to discuss Gavin right now. He'd made the decision to stay away, and Adam could only hope that if he needed help, he'd ask for it.

After finishing up dinner and helping with the dishes, Adam told his parents and Grace goodbye. Grace, for her part, was still annoyed with him, but thankfully, his little sister wasn't one to hold grudges. His mom hugged him, while Carl instructed him to do what he needed to do to save the vineyard. As if he needed to be told that, but Adam had nodded before making his way outside.

The sun was just setting, fireflies dancing about in the grass as cicadas sang in the trees. Adam had to admit he loved this time of year, with the long days and warm nights. Sure, the mosquitoes were annoying—he slapped at his arm when he heard one buzzing—but nothing was perfect. Not Heron's Landing, or River's Bend, or himself.

With that jolly thought, he drove back through the town, stopping at Mike's general store for a few things. Mike owned the only grocery store in Heron's Landing, and it also featured a small café and hardware section as well. Picking up pasta, tomatoes, and a few other items—no Hot Pockets this time, damn Grace—Adam was about to check out when he spotted a flash of color in his peripheral vision.

"Adam!" a voice called, and he turned to see Joy McGuire walking up to him. She wore a loose t-shirt above very short shorts, her legs lithe and milky white in the light of the store. She had little makeup on, and Adam found himself even more intrigued by her as a result. He liked her tendency toward color, but seeing her more subdued in this way made him feel like he was seeing a Joy not too many people got to see. A relaxed Joy, he thought.

"Miss McGuire," he said in reply.

She wrinkled her nose, her hands on her hips. "Are you seriously still going to call me that? You can call me Joy, you know. You won't explode if you do."

He knew that. But saying her name out loud was an intimacy he didn't want to cross. "Miss McGuire" was a woman who'd just moved into town who he'd met only a few times.

"Joy" was a woman he'd looked at with desire in his eyes and who he wanted to toss over his shoulder and take home with him.

So, "Miss McGuire" it was.

He noticed powdered donuts in her hand, plus a large bottle of Coke. "Is that your dinner?"

She glanced at the food, and then laughed. "Yeah, kind of. I'm too lazy to make anything right now. And for some reason I just needed some sugar. Don't tell anyone, though, okay? I'm supposed to be a sophisticated city girl who only eats organic kale and freshly squeezed carrot juice."

"I won't tell anyone," he said seriously. And at her look of surprise, he shifted in embarrassment, especially as silence stretched between them.

Why couldn't he talk to this woman? He wasn't some ladies' man like Jaime, but he could generally make conversation without spontaneously combusting. He'd talked to Carolyn enough that she'd married him, right? His heart contracted, remembering his dead wife, who wouldn't be waiting for him when he came home. Wouldn't smile at him as he got into bed and then turn to him with a laugh as he gathered her into his arms. Instead, he was talking to this woman, who was the antithesis of Carolyn, trying to say something...what? Flirtatious?

Disgusted with himself, he said something like a goodbye before paying for his things and leaving. And then he was disgusted with himself for an entirely new reason at the memory of the look on Joy's face, which had been one of hurt and surprise. Could he do nothing but offend this woman? He wasn't trying to be a jackass, but that seemed to be his modus operandi with her as of late.

About to get into his car, the evening sky now turned to purple twilight, Adam heard steps coming up to his car.

"So I gotta ask: did I do something to offend you? Or are you always this nice to new people in this town?" Joy had her hands on her hips, her head cocked to the side, and she looked so much like an inquisitive bird that he half expected feathers to sprout from her arms.

He struggled for an answer. Should he just say yes and drive off? But looking at her, he couldn't leave it at that. "No, I'm not," he said finally.

"No, you are always this nice? Or you aren't always this nice?"

Her words twisted around his brain. What was it about this woman that tied him up in knots? "No, I'm generally...nice."

"Oh, well," she replied as she crossed her arms. "I'm glad I'm special then."

Her defensive posture—no longer the curious bird—caused his chest to squeeze. Without thinking, he touched her arm, leaving his hand there for a moment. She gazed up at him, her mouth slightly agape.

"I don't know why we keep getting off on the wrong foot," he said slowly. "But as Grace likes to remind me, it's mostly my fault."

He hadn't removed his hand, and he had the sudden thought that he didn't want to. That was when she uncrossed her arms, and they moved down to her sides, as if they had a will of their own. His fingers brushed at the skin where her t-shirt ended.

"Did you use the aloe vera?" he asked gruffly.

She stared at him. Stared at his fingers on her arm. "Yes,"

she said softly. "Thank you. It really helped. The burn's almost gone already."

He couldn't see the color of her skin in the darkening twilight, but he could feel its heat underneath his fingertips. And he could smell her—roses, he thought—and with the fireflies blinking around them, it seemed as if they had been transported to an entirely new world. But he knew this wasn't a new world, and he took his hand away with a reluctance that shocked him.

"I'm glad. You should be more careful about getting sunburned," he said finally.

Her face transformed then into a bright smile, and she laughed. "You'd think I would've figured that out by now, but I guess not. But I stocked up—just for you."

At those words—"just for you"—Adam's heart stopped, and he felt as if this moment could go on for a lifetime. Just them two, alone, standing in front of each other. Gazing at each other and memorizing the other's faces, like doing otherwise were impossible. And that was when he bent down, wanting to press his lips to her to see if she tasted of roses, too, and then the jingle of the front door bell sounded, and they jumped away from each other.

"I'm closing up, Joy!" Mike called. "You have your key?"

"I'm good. Thanks, Mike!" she replied, her voice only slightly breathy.

The moment now shattered, Adam's only thought was that he needed to leave. He needed to escape this woman's spell on him. "I'll see you later," he said, opening his car door.

She blinked at him. "Okay," she said, "see you."

And then he drove off, forcing himself not to look behind him at Joy's shrinking figure.

CHAPTER FIVE

Two weeks after arriving in Heron's Landing, Joy fulfilled her promise to Grace and invited her over for a full-on girls' night. It included manicures, cocktails, and a variety of chick flicks—*10 Things I Hate About You* for Joy, and *Sleepless in Seattle* for Grace. Joy also tossed in a few random contenders to spice things up—*Terminator 2* and *Rocky*—mostly so she could tell people that girls' nights didn't mean they could only talk about boys and boy-related issues. Always important to pass the Bechdel Test in real life.

Pulling out the red polish to begin work on her nails, Joy squinted as she started on her left hand. Sadly, Dana the stylist was on maternity leave for the foreseeable future and didn't want to inhale nail polish fumes right now, so Joy was stuck doing her own manicures for now. Which was fine, but she wasn't talented enough to paint tiny flowers on her own nails, so they inevitably seemed rather plain in comparison to what she was used to.

Oh, the sacrifices she made coming to this town!

"Adam told me you went to River's Bend recently," Grace said as she went to go pop another bag of popcorn.

Joy didn't look up from painting her nails, mostly because she didn't want to let Grace know she had *feelings* about that whole...thing. Nope, no feelings tonight. Just frivolity and Bloody Mary's and girl stuff. At this point, she'd rather talk about periods than about Adam Danvers, but alas, Grace didn't seem to agree.

"He said you wanted to do a story about the vineyard. I hope he didn't run you off with a pitchfork for suggesting it. He's weird about journalists, you know." Grace came back over to the couch, setting the bowl of popcorn on the coffee table. Joy grabbed a few kernels with her unpainted hand, but one missed her mouth and bounced into the depths of the couch.

She then looked at Grace—oh yeah, Adam. The vineyard. Stories. Aloe vera.

Continuing to paint, she said in as airy a voice as she could manage: "He didn't run me off, but he wasn't exactly welcoming of the idea, either. He does realize there's a thing called the First Amendment, where I can write what I want despite what Adam Danvers thinks?" She swiped the side of her ring finger with the nail polish brush, and she sighed. "I mean, it's not like I'd write something that would cause him to sue me for libel. Generally, people don't sue writers for *positive* stories about their business."

Grace laughed. "Adam wouldn't sue you. He's just...cranky. Plus, the vineyard's been struggling for a while, so I know that's stressed him out a lot."

Her ears perking up suddenly, Joy found herself leaning forward to hear more. It wasn't any of her business, but the damned nosy writer/bloodhound inside of her loved this kind of information. She also—despite her internal protestations otherwise—wanted to know more about Adam. What made him tick? Why did he look perpetually constipated? How did he get his dark hair so perfectly wavy?

"Why is it struggling? Bad harvest?" Joy switched over to her right hand, painting her thumbnail the crimson red with slow strokes.

"That, and the weather has sucked for the past three years. My dad always thought global warming was a hoax until it began wrecking the business. Last year there was a drought, and before that, tons of rain. Same thing this year: rain, rain, and more rain." Grace sighed as she leaned back into the couch. "We've talked to him about doing events again, but he's stubborn. He doesn't want to change things."

Joy nodded. She could see Adam being stubborn as hell while also being resistant to change. Whereas she liked to shake things up as often as possible—she moved to this teeny town, for Christ's sake—he seemed like he'd hate moving to a big city. Or even a medium city. She couldn't really fault him for planting such deep roots here, and a small part of her envied him that.

"I thought you guys already did events," Joy said, thinking about the wine-tasting class she'd seen going on when she'd gone to the vineyard. "Do you mean like parties?"

"No, more like weddings. We tried to do weddings a few years ago when Dad was still the manager, but it didn't work out so well." Grace wrinkled her nose. "I know that after that, Adam basically swore off ever trying it again. But Jaime says that it's probably one of the best bets to bring in revenue..."

Her voice trailed off, and Joy glanced up to see the younger woman biting her lip.

After spending only a small amount of time with Grace Danvers, Joy had discovered two things: the girl was a brilliant artist but lacked confidence in her own talents, and she was also madly in love with the chef of River's Bend, Jaime Martínez. Joy had only seen Jaime a few times from a distance, but she couldn't fault the girl for her taste. He was handsome, tall, and could cook, and he probably saved orphans and nursed puppies in his spare time. If Joy weren't already preoccupied with her own mess of a life, she'd go after Jaime herself. Well, and if Grace weren't making goo-goo eyes at him every chance she got.

Enjoying this change in subject, Joy screwed the cap back on the nail polish and sat back into the couch. "How is Jaime, by the way?" she asked with a smile.

Grace immediately grabbed a fistful of popcorn, which she ate kernel by kernel in some attempt to avoid Joy's question. Finally, probably knowing she was being rude, she said, "He's fine, I guess. I don't see him much since he's always working. Why do you ask?"

Joy waved her hand to air dry her nails. "No reason. Just that I've noticed you seem to watch him anytime he's around. Yesterday you stopped speaking to me for at least five minutes when he entered Trudy's."

"I did not."

"Mmmm, pretty sure you did. And then when I thought you'd at least tell the man good morning, you scurried off into the back like he had the plague." Seeing that Grace was getting agitated, Joy knew she shouldn't tease her too much longer. "Have you ever thought about asking him out?"

Grace's eyes widened so much that, clearly, the idea had never come to mind. "What? No. Why would I? He's my brother's employee. No, I couldn't." She grabbed more popcorn, eating it so quickly Joy was half-afraid she'd choke on it.

"Well, you like him, obviously. Seems natural you'd see if it could go anywhere."

Silence fell, with only the sound of Grace chewing in the room. They hadn't yet put on a movie—and Joy almost got up to do so to give Grace a respite—but then the girl blurted, "It wouldn't matter anyway. He's only ever seen me as Adam's little sister."

Ah, that explained it, Joy thought. Getting up, she popped *Sleepless in Seattle* from its DVD case and placed it into the player. Sitting back down, she said, "You'll never know if you don't try," she said simply.

Grace didn't reply, but Joy knew she was mulling over her words the rest of the evening.

Joy, for her part, couldn't concentrate on the movies, but instead couldn't stop thinking about Adam, River's Bend, and the vineyard potentially shutting down. That vineyard had to be one of the bigger sources of revenue for Heron's Landing, and if it shut down, she was sure the town would end up hurting as a result. It attracted tourists from all over the state and the country. She didn't really understand why Adam was resistant to doing events, but maybe he felt like he couldn't do it without assistance?

An idea sprang to mind. She was no events coordinator, but she knew enough about marketing and social media to lend a hand. Plus, if she wrote about the vineyard doing weddings and had it published in a nationwide magazine? Jackpot.

She began filing away ideas in her mind, thinking about who'd she'd contact about writing the story, and how she'd go about getting Adam to see the light. Perhaps if she just went ahead and did it, he'd see the positive results and go from there? Her logical side said that he'd probably be furious if she went behind his back, but that didn't mean she couldn't *plan* behind his back, either.

Joy had a deep need to be useful to those around her, and in the two weeks she'd been in Heron's Landing, she'd only gotten so far as to interview Mike in the general store about a new kind of grape he was stocking. It wasn't breaking news or Nobel-prize winning journalism, but she liked that she was writing about things that a few people in the town would like to be aware existed. After getting as much out of Mike as she could—the man was of few words, and it was like pulling teeth to get him to say complete sentences—she'd written a short article, titled "Heron's Landing Great New Grape." Not her best work, but hey, she could generate some revenue from Google ads at the end of the day, too.

The article had gone up this morning on the newly created Heron's Landing blog, while Joy had also verbally told as many townsfolk as she could about the new online publication. Most people were nonplussed, while a few of the younger people were interested, but again, it was a start. Joy didn't plan on making tons of money, and her other freelance gigs were paying the rent, but she liked to think she was making her mark on this small town all the same.

Grace soon overcame her mood and became the bright, bubbly young woman who Joy was rather enjoying having as a friend already. And thankfully, she'd agreed to call Joy by her first name. Joy felt a little guilty teasing her about Jaime —who knew how deep that infatuation went?—but obviously, Grace wasn't one to hold grudges or get easily offended.

When Grace was leaving, though, she said in a soft voice, "Sometimes I don't think I know what I want to do."

Joy, standing at the front door, didn't know how to respond. She preferred to keep things light and funny, not serious. But Grace's face was taut with some emotion Joy couldn't identify.

"You'll figure it out," Joy said with as much assurance as she could. "You're young: you have your entire life to figure things out."

Grace smiled sadly before she turned to go. She said a goodbye, but Joy wondered how much of her words were about Jaime, or about her life in general. Sometimes Joy saw a kind of loneliness in Grace that surprised her, and even a lostness of sorts. Despite the bubbly exterior, something else simmered underneath.

Joy closed her door, leaning against it with a sigh. She had a feeling she was getting in over her head with the ever-increasingly complicated Danvers family.

WHY WON'T you return my calls?

Joy glanced at the text from Jeremy and almost blocked his number entirely. He'd texted her twice previously, and now he wouldn't let up. What did even want from her? He was the one who'd cheated, not her.

Cranky and tired, she replied, *Because you cheated on me and I don't want to talk to you? I'm not sure why this is so complicated.*

She probably shouldn't antagonize him—sometimes she thought Jeremy loved fighting as much as anything—but she was tired of this. She'd left Chicago for a number of reasons, and having one of those big reasons still dogging her steps didn't help her mood at all.

The three dots appeared, and then: *I don't get why you won't talk to me at all. I'm trying here, Jo-Jo.*

She snorted. Trying so hard that he cheated on her with her best friend Regina? Yeah, that sure was trying very, very hard. But Jeremy hated when people ignored him, and he still thought he had a right to be in Joy's life despite everything. Thus, the incessant texting.

Jeremy had been fun and kind and hilarious in the beginning. But after a year or two, he became increasingly paranoid about her cheating on him, which ironically turned out to be the reverse situation. What had been a charming devil-may-care attitude had evolved into a cloying immaturity as Jeremy got older. Then, as accusation after accusation of Joy cheating piled up, their relationship suffered, and they were on the verge of breaking up when the bombshell came: Jeremy had slept with Regina and he was leaving Joy for her.

To say that Joy hadn't reacted well would be an understatement.

Leave me alone. I don't want to talk, okay? Can you respect that for once? she texted.

Nothing. And then: *I know you think it was all my fault, but you need to take responsibility, too. We both fucked up.*

Anger surged. He was really blaming *her* for him cheating? She'd laugh at his unmitigated gall if she weren't so pissed.

She may not have been always the happy, supportive girl-friend, but she'd never betrayed Jeremy, either.

Her fingers furiously typing, she sent him a terse, *Leave me alone or I'm blocking your number* before she turned her phone off. She didn't care if someone needed to get a hold of her. They'd live.

Staring at the walls of her apartment, she suddenly couldn't stay inside for one more second. Tossing her phone onto the couch, she grabbed her keys and walked outside. The sun had already set, twilight seeping through the dark green trees. Fireflies danced around her, and she'd admire how idyllic the town seemed at this hour if she weren't so angry.

She stomped down a path toward a creek she'd found a few days before, her fists clenched and a scream choking her. She wished she could just stand in the middle of the forest and scream her throat raw, kicking her feet like she would when she was a little kid throwing a temper tantrum. The anger was so raw, so overwhelming, she didn't even see where she was going. It only increased with every step, a variety of voices pushing each other inside of her mind.

Fuck Jeremy! I hope he dies in a fire!

He's such a fucking narcissist he'd blame his own mother for committing a murder.

God, I can't believe I dated him and was going to marry him.

And the worst of all: what if she could've prevented him from cheating in the first place?

Standing at the creek, she stared into the trees and watched the fireflies and breathed and breathed until a sob ricocheted from her throat. Tears flooded her eyes, and she swiped at her face. She'd always been an angry crier, and she was so angry she didn't know if she could cry enough tears to purge the rage inside of her.

I hate him I hate him I hate him. She hated him and she hated herself. She cried for what they'd had and maybe for the fact that they'd never had anything to begin with. Sitting down on the bank with her arms around her knees, she cried her heart out until she was snotty and her face was soaked and so were her knees. She was glad it was so dark, although she wondered how she'd get back home without breaking her neck on some tree root.

"Hey, are you okay?"

Light from a phone flashed on her feet, and Joy jumped. She scrambled up, but not before scraping her hands on some rocks. She cursed.

"Miss McGuire? What are you doing out here?" The dark figure came closer, and she realized, not with surprise but resignation, that it was Adam Danvers. Of course it was. "Are you okay?" he asked again.

"I'm fine," she replied in clipped tones.

He stood only a few feet from her, but it was dark enough that she couldn't see his face.

Then: "Are you sure? Do you want me to help you back home?"

"No," she said. "I don't need your help, and I don't need men constantly thinking I need them to hold my hand like I'm some delicate flower." She knew she was ranting like a loon, but she didn't care. He thought she was crazy, anyway.

She swiped her hands down her shorts, hissing in a breath at the pain. She couldn't see, but she could bet she'd done a number on her hands.

Adam stepped closer, and before she realized it, he'd taken

her hands in his. He'd placed his lit-up phone in his front pocket, and it provided just enough illumination now for her to see his face. "You're bleeding," he said.

"I fell."

"Clearly."

And then he looked at her face, and she hoped against hope he couldn't see that she'd been crying. Although he'd probably heard her sobbing like a toddler.

He didn't let go of her hands, holding them gently in his much larger ones. Joy felt the calluses on his fingertips and how warm his hands were. The moment expanded, like it had outside of Mike's store only a few days prior. That electricity sparked between them, and she shivered despite herself.

"Miss McGuire," Adam said in a low voice. And then to her surprise, "Joy."

Her heart pounded. She wanted him to kiss her, with a sudden desperation that shocked her. She wanted him to pull her close and kiss her until she forgot everything about this day.

As if sensing her need, he let go of one of her hands and cupped her cheek. His thumb stroked her face, and her eyelashes fluttered, her eyes closing.

When he finally kissed her, she wondered if there could be a moment as pure, as crystalline, as fantastical as this one. With the fireflies around them, the cicadas humming, the breeze twirling the leaves in the trees overhead. But all of that dissipated like a breath in a storm when his mouth touched hers. His lips were soft, warm, and he kissed her with soft-lipped kisses that made her melt.

The kisses were like a question—is this what you want? he seemed to be asking.

She twined her arms around his neck, answering him.

Yes, this is what I want, she thought.

They kissed until time stopped, mouths moving against one another in exploration. Joy's heart pounded so hard she felt dizzy, and she was glad she had his solid form to hang onto. Pressing against him, she kissed him harder, and he soon took the lead. His tongue tangled with hers, and the kisses became deeper and deeper. She felt like he was subsuming her entire being. It was heady, glorious.

Terrifying.

When they parted, neither said anything. Eventually, he pulled away and said, "Let's get you home."

She nodded, letting him lead her home without once doubting he'd get her there safely.

CHAPTER SIX

Adam had hoped that the sunshine of the past few weeks would hold up until the harvest. But on a Monday morning in early July, he awoke to claps of thunder. Getting out of bed, he opened the blinds to see torrential rain falling like bullets from the sky. Hail pinged the roof, and a bolt of lightning burst across the sky.

The rain continued all day. It stopped for a bit in the evening, but started up again by Tuesday morning. By Wednesday, it had rained so hard that flash flood warnings had been issued across the state, and the river was about to flood from its banks. There was so much water that the unpaved roads around Heron's Landing—and there were plenty of them—turned to mud, and many of its citizens had to stay home or walk to their destination, as any vehicle would get stuck the moment it was put in drive.

By Wednesday afternoon, the sun had come out, but Adam knew it was too late. Going into the fields with Jaime and a few others of his staff, they all saw how the rain had deci-mated the remaining buds. The delicate petals scattered across the ground, a small hope crushed. Bending down, Adam fingered a few of the waterlogged buds, breathing through his nose in an attempt to calm his pounding heart.

No one said anything. What was there to say? Everyone knew what this would mean for the harvest. No buds meant no grapes meant no wine. Some of the hardiest buds had managed to hang on, but there was so little white remaining on the vines that Adam didn't know how the harvest could be salvaged.

Jaime came to stand by him, placing a hand on his shoulder. "We'll figure it out," he said quietly.

Adam had to restrain himself from snapping back. But he knew his friend meant well, and that he'd do anything to help River's Bend and Adam. Standing up, he replied, "I guess we'll have to, won't we?"

Leah, a middle-aged woman who did the wine-tasting classes part-time, walked along the rows of vines, clicking her tongue. A small-statured woman with a sharp tongue, she generally considered any event like this one of God's divine retribution. Devoted to the church, she'd never married, but preferred to read her Bible and come out to Heron's Landing to show unsuspecting tourists how they had no idea how to drink and appreciate wine properly. Today, though, she said nothing, and Adam knew that that wasn't a good sign. Leah always had an opinion.

The day was sticky with humidity, and he slapped a mosquito off of his arm. Continuing to wander along the rows, he found one length of vine that was mostly intact. It was a small hope, in the grand scheme of things, but seeing those white buds bursting from the vines felt like the greatest of victories. At least there was something. At least they could harvest a few grapes. It wouldn't be nearly enough, but Adam was determined not to despair entirely.

Later inside, closeted with his employees, Adam went over their options. "As you all could see for yourselves, the weather this year has not been kind to us. Without buds, there are no grapes. And you already know what that means. If this had been just this year, we could've salvaged things." He swallowed, thinking about the previous two years of bad harvest. His temples throbbed, and he wished he could go home and drink until all of his worries faded away in a haze of liquor.

The employees present were only a handful—Kerry, Jaime, Leah, and Chris, who was the overseer of the harvesters come the fall. But they made up a hard-working, bright group of people, and Adam was glad that he had them to rely upon.

"Do we have any idea how much the harvest will actually yield?" Chris asked. A man close to Adam's father's age, Chris had salt-and-pepper hair with a neatly trimmed beard. His skin was the tanned skin of a man often out in the sun, although his wife had been bugging him about wearing more sunscreen as of late. After reading about the depletion of the ozone layer, she'd been scared to death that Chris would develop melanoma; Chris, for his part, preferred to ignore his wife's arguments and do as he pleased.

Adam shook his head at Chris's comment. "We'll have to wait and see how many of the buds turn into actual grapes. But I can say that the harvest will have been depleted by two-thirds, just by looking at the vines."

The group inhaled all at once at the number. They glanced around at each other before Kerry spoke, her voice tentative. "So the harvest is bad. What about doing events, like we'd discussed before?"

Leah glared at Kerry—she wasn't fond of events like Adam—while Chris scratched at his chin. Jaime, undeterred, said, "It sounds like that's our only option now. We're not bringing in the revenue in the restaurant itself, we're not bringing in the revenue from the wine-tasting classes—sorry, Leah, but it's true—and now that we aren't going to be selling as much wine, we need some other source. Simple as that."

Adam gritted his teeth. Jaime was right, and he knew he was right. He didn't want him to be right, but such was life. Memories of the disaster of the last time they'd tried to do events filled his mind, and he rather wanted to say no and end it there. Couldn't they find another way? A voice in his head niggled. Something, anything?

But looking at Jaime, who had an eyebrow raised, Adam knew that denying the obvious would be absolutely foolish. He sighed inwardly—his last sigh of defeat—and pushed all of his misgivings aside. Doubts wouldn't help anyone, and they sure as hell wouldn't help River's Bend survive.

"You all know events aren't my strong suit," Adam said. Jaime snorted; Adam glared. "So I'll need everyone's help with planning and getting it running. Unfortunately, we don't have the cash flow to hire a full-time events manager, so it's going to fall on all of us to do bits and pieces and make it work."

"I'm not an events manager," Leah said bluntly. "I can teach the wine-tasting like usual, but working with brides and such? No way."

As if to cushion Leah's words, Kerry said quickly, "I can help with any social media and marketing, and reach out to any local blogs and sites to get things rolling."

"Thank you, Kerry," Adam said. They needed more than a

few Facebook posts to get this started, but having at least one employee on board was helpful.

The afternoon and evening waned on as the team put together a competent strategy, going over what went wrong the first time around and how to avoid such mistakes again. Each employee—including Leah—was given tasks of a sort; even Chris, who preferred to be outdoors at all times had things he needed to do. The majority of it landed on Adam, though, which he had expected as the vineyard's manager. If he needed to work eighty hours a week and never go home, he'd do it.

Afterward, Jaime met Adam at his truck, everyone else had already gone home for the night. It wasn't dark yet, but twilight was settling in. Adam saw that Jaime looked tired, and he hated that in the next coming weeks, he and everyone else on staff would only have to work longer hours with no overtime pay. He'd explained that he couldn't pay them and that he didn't expect them to work, but all four had agreed without protest—even Leah.

"You think it'll work?" Jaime asked.

Adam leaned against the driver's side door of his truck, rubbing his forehead. "If I were honest? I don't know. I want it to. I want to hope that we can get out of this black hole. But it's a long shot."

Jaime stuffed his hands into his pockets. "I didn't want to say this in the meeting, but I talked to Joy this morning when she came by, when you were still out in the field."

At the mention of Joy, Adam stilled, memories resurfacing. All of it flooded back in an instant, and he was reliving that kiss—every facet of it. He hadn't intended to kiss her when he'd found her down by the creek. But she'd looked so beautiful, almost ethereal, standing amongst the blinking lightning bugs, that it was like he'd had no choice. He shifted, feeling himself react to the memory of that kiss, of Joy's sweet smell and taste and the silk of her skin.

Jaime just watched him, and Adam coughed, embarrassed by his daydreaming. "Why was she here?"

"Well, she wanted to talk. To me."

Adam raised an eyebrow. "To you? Do you even know her?"

Jaime smiled. "She's the type of person who knows everyone. I think she knew everyone's names—first, middle and last—by the third day after she'd arrived."

A bite of jealousy burned in Adam's gut, and, annoyed with himself, he pushed it away. What did it matter that Joy was talking to other people in Heron's Landing? Even if it was Jaime Martínez, blindingly handsome chef extraordinaire (per Grace, earlier that week).

"So, she did what? Told you her life story and then you guys sang around the campfire?"

"Not exactly. She asked me about the vineyard, how it was doing. And then she told me she was working on a story about it."

Adam froze. Hadn't she promised him she wouldn't write a story without consulting him?

Jaime continued, "I know how you are about journalists. I don't agree with it, but I know that you'd want to know. I told her nothing that isn't already known, but she seemed to imply that she could publish it within a week or two. Specifically, it would focus on the vineyard doing events again, to draw interest, she said."

There it is, Adam thought. *That's the reason behind it all.* On the surface it may have seemed like a nice way to help River's Bend, but he knew journalists enough to know that it was all about site hits and ad revenue. Plus, Adam hadn't publicly announced anything about them doing events, and having someone unrelated to the vineyard driving the brand? It was, in a word, infuriating.

"I told her not to do anything without talking to me," Adam finally ground out.

"Look, I knew you wouldn't be happy. But don't jump to conclusions. She seems like a good person, and I think she genuinely wants to help."

"We don't need her help. And she's doing something expressly against what I asked." Realizing he was taking out his anger on Jaime, Adam said in a level tone, "I'm not going to storm into her place right this second. But if she thinks she's going to get away with it, she has another thing coming."

Jaime sighed, running his hands through his hair. "Just, think on it, okay? Don't do anything fucking stupid. You're already stressed and angry. I know it, we all know it."

Adam knew Jaime was speaking sense, but he wasn't in the mood to hear it. Opening the truck door, he climbed inside, turning on the engine. "I'll see you later, Jaime."

Jaime stepped out of the way of the truck, and Adam reversed and drove away with Jaime shaking his head in the rearview mirror.

Driving home in his large truck, which was one of the few vehicles that could successfully drive on the muddy roads, Adam couldn't stop shaking his head. Had that kiss meant nothing to Joy? He fumed and clenched the steering wheel, restraining himself from punching the horn. Did she not care that he'd asked her for basic consideration? Why was that so much to ask? So what if it seemed extreme? It was his business, his vineyard, and he had a right to control what was said about it.

When he arrived home, he pressed his forehead to the steering wheel, breathing deeply. His logical side told him he was overreacting. He knew it. He knew he was being ridiculous. But the entire thing—stories and journalists and using others for their own gain—made his stomach twist and his head throb. Memories of reporters banging on his door, seeing headlines splashed across the Internet, forced him to close his eyes.

Adam hadn't always been against journalists. In fact, he'd supported them as much as anyone else, agreeing that the best ones were doing a civil service in uncovering the truth. Some were hacks working for an easy buck, but others placed themselves in danger for stories that needed to be told. Otherwise, they didn't factor into his life, any more than any other profession.

Until Carolyn. Carolyn Danvers, nee Young, had been a famous rich girl of the Young family, which owned a department store chain spread across the United States. She'd made a name for herself in her charity works, walking the biggest red carpets and becoming a household name. Along with her charity efforts, she cemented her fashion icon status quickly, wearing designers that Adam had never heard of and couldn't name to this day. How would he know who Alexander McQueen or Monique Lhuillier were?

But all of that ended when Carolyn had died in a car accident not far from their home three years ago, her car hitting a tree and killing her upon impact.

Inside his house—their house—he stared at their wedding

photo. She'd worn a deceptively simple gown that had cost more than the house he stood in. But he didn't see the gown: he saw her smile, and he saw his own. He'd adored her. And now, he missed her with a fierce, all-consuming ache.

After the accident, the reporters and journalists had hounded him. They'd dug deep into his history and hers, bringing up any possible sordid detail to be consumed by the fascinated public. An arrest when Adam had been seventeen and stupid, a shoplifting arrest when Carolyn had also been young and stupid. But it was when the headlines had turned vicious that Adam had had enough: he'd seen his family suffer enough from the constant barrage of whispers and questions and paranoia, fearing that someone would be listening and report their findings to the media. They could barely leave their house without being hounded.

Adam shook his head, shaking away the memories. He couldn't let them take hold of him again. Going into the kitchen, he grabbed the decanter of whiskey and poured himself more than enough for the night. He didn't normally drink much, but desperate times called for desperate measures. Slugging back the liquor, the burn of it slid down his throat, settling like a stone in his belly.

The night waned away as he drank more and more whiskey, his vision going hazy. Muttering to himself, he paced around the house. How dare Joy do something like that? How could she lie to his face? And after they'd kissed! He'd so stupidly thought there was something between them, despite their initial dislike, but apparently that had been a mere illusion. Had she let him kiss her to lull him into a false sense of security?

At the thought, he shuddered. He was becoming paranoid

again, like when Carolyn had died. He couldn't let himself go into that place again, when he was checking his house for wires like the goddamn CIA was on his trail and investigating him. Finishing off the whiskey, he went to the bathroom before falling into a restless sleep.

In the morning, he opened his eyes and groaned. His head pounded. How much had he drunk? He took a hot shower, trying to clear the cobwebs from his mind. When he checked his phone, he saw a text message from Jaime: *Don't do anything stupid.*

He replied, *Of course.*

Going through his contacts, he pressed his thumb on Joy's number. He listened to it ring, and ring, and ring, and then her voice saying, "Hello?"

"I need to see you. Are you available now?"

Silence. Then, "Uh, I guess so. I just woke up, though."

"Good. I'll be there in fifteen. See you at Trudy's."

CHAPTER SEVEN

Joy hadn't expected Adam would be thrilled about her doing a story on the vineyard. But she hadn't expected he'd be quite so steamed, either.

Sitting across from him in a booth at Trudy's, twenty minutes after he'd called and mysteriously asked to see her, she sipped her coffee, waiting for him to say something. Instead, he seemed intent on having a staring contest with her. If she'd known he just wanted to glare at her, she would've stayed in bed, made her own coffee and maybe watched a movie.

Feeling peevish and tired, she asked, "You wanted to talk to me about something?"

He ripped open a sugar packet with more force than strictly necessary, and thus the majority of the granules ended up on the table. He swore. "Are you writing a story about the vineyard?" he asked in clipped tones.

Joy sipped her coffee. Grace wasn't working today, and she could tell that Terry had made the coffee today because it tasted like bitter lukewarm water. She dumped more creamer in it, slowly stirring, watching Adam stew. She rather liked watching him stew.

How had the man sitting before her kissed her so tenderly not so long ago? It was like he'd been a completely different person that evening. One who didn't look like he'd murder puppies from his scowl alone.

She took another sip of coffee. Sighed. And then replied, "I am writing a story, because it's of interest to me and, I believe, to a lot of potential readers."

"And yet you're doing it without consulting me, which I expressly forbade you from doing?"

She burst out laughing. "'Expressly forbade?' Buddy, it's way too early to be using words like that."

He scowled, his expression rather thunderous. If Joy weren't so tired and cranky, she might be freaked out. Then again, she knew how men liked to bluster and bitch. No woman could match a man going on an emotional rampage.

"I asked you not to write it without consulting me, yet here you are, doing just that? Can you explain that?" He sat back, watching her.

"Wellllllll," she said slowly, "I realize I may have given the impression that I was doing what you wanted. But then I thought, 'This guy isn't my boss and it's a free country.' So, I decided to do the story regardless. First Amendment, you know."

"Just because you can doesn't mean you should."

She shrugged. A little bit of guilt niggled at her for her white lie, but Adam had no right to dictate what she could or could not write and publish. She wasn't writing anything negative. For God's sake, it was a positive piece to bring in potential tourists, which meant money! Who turned down money?

"Look, you can be pissy and moan-y all you want. But you should know that this piece is completely positive and was meant to *help* you. It ain't libel in the slightest. So calm your titties and drink your coffee."

"Are you always this pleasant?"

"Only to jackasses who try to fuck me over." She smiled widely. Now she was really cranky. Why did men continue to think they could mess with her and get away with it? The mascara didn't equate to stupidity, but it was the story of her life that men underestimated her anyway.

"I'm not trying to fuck you over," Adam said, leaning toward her, his voice low. "I just would like anything written about my business to have my eyes on it first. Surely you understand that."

"Sure I do. But that's also code for wanting to control a narrative entirely, and I'm wholly uninterested in playing that game. And if you thought about what I was doing for five seconds, you'd realize it would only help you in the end."

He laughed, a little stunned. His initial scowl had faded, and he seemed to be looking at her with sheer incredulity. She could work with that, generally speaking, as she was used to it.

"Is that what you're doing?" he asked. "You're helping me by using my business for your own means?"

Joy threw her hands up in the air. "Oh my God! Yes, I'm writing a story to pay my bills! Call the police, Adam, and arrest me for being like everyone else in this damn country." She rubbed her temples; stubborn men gave her the worst kinds of headaches.

"If you had any kind of integrity, you'd do as I asked and actually honor your promise."

She stilled. "Now you're just insulting me." Anger began pulsing through her, and it took everything she had in her to restrain herself from tossing her coffee in his face.

He looked smug, the bastard. "No, I'm pointing out the obvious. Do the right thing and we can end this right here."

Clenching her mug between her hands, Joy fell silent. She'd put up with a lot in her life—including receiving blame for things not entirely her fault—and she could hear Jeremy's words to her: *If you'd loved me more, I wouldn't have cheated.* If she'd tried harder, been nicer, put everyone else before her own needs at all times, been sweet and thoughtful and demure. If she'd had *integrity.*

She wasn't going to apologize for writing what she wanted. She wasn't going to apologize for not asking permission to write what she wanted. And she sure as hell wasn't going to back down because Adam Danvers was the biggest asshole this side of the Mississippi River.

"You know the funny thing about me?" She looked up at him, forcing her voice to be calm. Measured. Emotions were a woman's worst enemy in these types of battles.

"What?"

"That when anyone tries to get me to do something simply because they're a jackass, it gives me more of a reason to do it anyway." Standing, she grabbed her purse and looked down at Adam, who was just staring at her. "Oh, and you know what else? I talked to people in Chicago about helping with the events at River's Bend. Because that's what friends do—help each other. But you're so intent on seeing things as some master plot to screw you over, that you lose anyone who might actually be a friend."

He said nothing, but she could see his fist clenching at his side. "What are you saying?" he ground out.

"I'm saying that I'm going to write whatever the hell I want, and you can eat a dick. Toodles."

She stalked out of the café, leaving Adam with the measly coffee bill. She began walking back to her apartment, but the thought of sitting up there sounded so unbearable that she stalked off in the direction of the creek. She also didn't want to talk to Mike, or anyone else in the general store. She waited to hear Adam come after her, but he didn't.

Hurt filled her, and she could feel tears threatening. She swiped at them. She was an angry crier, and God above, she was angry. Angry at herself for thinking Adam was a good guy despite her first impression of him, angry at herself for kissing him! But mostly she was angry that he thought she was such a heartless jerk that she'd screw him over for her own gain. She was a fucking journalist, not some Wall Street big wig stealing money from the poor to line her own pockets. Hell, she barely made anything in the last few weeks because she'd been preoccupied with life and moving.

If you had any integrity—the words bounced around in her mind until she was close to chucking her purse and stomping on it out of sheer rage. Instead, she kicked a tree, and then swore at the pain radiating up her foot from the attempt. Could her life be more of a mess?

She finally walked to a log overlooking the creek. She sat down with a plop, huffing out a breath. The tears had mostly disappeared, but she probably looked a sight: flushed and scowling and swearing underneath her breath. She wished she could be a subtle person when angry, but that had never been her style. But once she got it out of her system, she generally moved on.

Adam Danvers can suck a dick and I hope he falls off a cliff and dies. To occupy herself, she imagined terrible, ridiculous fates for him—getting eaten alive by raccoons, choking on a sandwich, getting the plague—before she calmed down enough to think a little more clearly.

The wind whistled through the trees, and Joy watched as birds flitted about in the branches. She spotted a bright red cardinal in one of the shrubs. She smiled, watching it hop around. She soon spotted a female cardinal, more brown then red, and realized there was probably a nest in the shrub. She smiled a little sadly.

A small voice in her head told her she'd gotten herself into this bind by agreeing with Adam but then reneging, but she pushed that voice aside. She wasn't in the mood to understand him. He had insulted her, and she didn't have time to be nice to whiny man babies. Jeremy had been the whiniest of man babies at the end, crying about how she'd never loved him.

Was there anything worse in this world than whiny man babies? Joy didn't think so.

She sat on the log for a few hours, just staring off into the distance. She probably should get back, work on a story, pay her bills. Figure out her life, ignore that she'd been falling for Adam and now she hated everything about him. Was that to be her fate with men? Fall for them and then when they showed their true colors, wish instead that they'd get hit by a tractor and be run over multiple times, very slowly?

"Joy?"

Turning, Joy saw Grace walking toward her. The girl had

her hair in a braid down her back, and she looked rather like a fairy princess come to reunite with her woodland subjects. Joy's heart clenched, though, seeing how much Grace looked like her brother. They had the same eyes, she realized.

She looked away.

"I heard what happened," Grace said, sitting beside her. "Do you want to talk about it?"

"Not really."

Grace fidgeted, pulling at random threads on her white dress. "I'm sorry about all of this. Adam can be such a jerk sometimes."

"Only sometimes?"

"He's a good guy," Grace pressed. Joy looked over at her, and saw the seriousness in her expression. "He's just...stubborn."

"Stubborn enough to say that I have no integrity and am basically a terrible person?"

Wincing, Grace looked away. "I didn't realize he'd said that, exactly. I just ran into him after he left Trudy's, and he was so steamed that I couldn't get much out of him."

"Well, if anyone should be steamed, it's me. I didn't completely insult him and then make ridiculous demands." Her anger rising again, she continued, "You know, I tried to like your brother. I did. We didn't start off very well, but I wasn't going to hold that against him. And then what happened down at the creek here—"

"What happened here?"

Joy blushed, remembering. She'd remember that kiss until her dying day. If she didn't hate Adam so much right now, she'd go find him and kiss him again just to experience it again. It had been like no other kiss she'd ever had—and she'd had some good kisses in her lifetime. At the beginning of their relationship, she and Jeremy couldn't keep their hands off of each other. But the kiss with Adam hadn't just been about desire; if Joy thought about it too much, she'd freak herself out.

"Nothing happened," Joy replied shortly. She could see Grace staring at her, and when she caught her gaze, the girl smiled.

"Nothing? Why are you blushing? Oh my God, did you guys sleep together?"

Joy squawked. "Jesus Christ! No! And why are you asking questions like that about your brother? And who would have sex in the dirt by a creek? That's the most country thing I've ever heard."

"You're deflecting."

"No, I'm telling you you're losing your marbles. And besides, even if we'd pledged our undying love for each other, that doesn't negate that your brother is, in fact, a complete jackass."

The two women fell silent. Grace placed her hands in her lap, her fingernails still a bright red from their girls' night manicure session. In a quiet voice, she said, "I didn't come here to excuse my brother's actions. But I also wanted you to know that there's more to the story than you might realize."

Joy didn't want to be persuaded. She didn't want to hear Adam's sob story. She didn't want to let go of her anger and understand things. She wanted to stay mad and trip him when she saw him walking down the street.

Sometimes a girl just wanted to stay petty.

"I told you his wife Carolyn died, right?" Grace continued. "He hasn't been the same since." At Joy's look, she added, "I'm not giving that as an excuse. But it's true. He's been...angry, I think. He wasn't always like that."

"But what does that have to do with me writing a story about the vineyard?"

Grace inhaled, brushing a leaf from her dress. "I can't tell you all of the details, but I can say that there was a lot of media coverage when Carolyn died, and it was really painful for Adam. For all of us."

Joy swiveled toward Grace. "Media coverage? Why?"

"Carolyn was the daughter of Trenton Young, the founder of Young & Co." At Joy's eyes widening, Grace said, "She was a sort of celebrity, especially around here."

Joy—and everyone else in the United States—knew exactly what Young & Co. was: a store where you could basically buy anything you needed at prices that were surely illegal. You couldn't go ten miles without seeing a Young & Co. store. Joy hadn't known anything about the family, but she found herself intrigued regardless. Adam had been married to a celebrity? Who knew?

"So when she died, people reported on it, and Adam got mad?" Joy frowned. "That seems like a flimsy excuse to hate all journalists from here to eternity."

"It would be, if that were the only reason." Grace smiled sadly. "I can't tell you anymore—I know, I know—because Adam asked that no one talk about it. I'm probably saying more than I should already. But suffice to say, he has his reasons. They may seem extreme, but sometimes when horrible things happen, we fight against whatever we can to preserve what we have left, you know?"

Joy fell silent at that. She marveled at this young woman— barely twenty-three years old—who could speak with such insight into human nature. Joy didn't particularly want to be persuaded, but she could feel her anger cooling despite herself. She was still mad, but it was an anger tinged with curiosity to know why.

After talking for a little while longer, Joy and Grace parted. Joy returned to her apartment, where she drummed her fingers on her coffee table in thought. Did she go down that rabbit hole or not? Giving herself a reason to understand Adam Danvers more could possibly backfire, but then again, curiosity killed the cat was her M.O. in all things.

Opening up her laptop, she Googled "Carolyn Danvers," receiving a number of hits regarding the accident and Carolyn's subsequent death. She read about the car crashing into a tree, and how Carolyn had been DOA when taken to the hospital. Joy winced at the photos of the crash site: the car looked like Godzilla had picked it up and smashed it between its claws, it was so mangled. The accident had been just that: an accident due to rainy weather.

Clicking through more articles, she read about Carolyn's various charities, her family's influence, articles condemning the labor practices of Young & Co. She read about Carolyn's days at Stanford as an undergraduate, and her marriage to Adam. She even found wedding photos of the two from seven years ago, and she was taken aback by how happy Adam looked. She'd never seen his face softened like that, almost bursting with love.

After that, she closed her laptop. Sitting back onto the couch, she couldn't help but feel sympathy for Adam and his entire family. To lose his wife in such a random, tragic way? They'd clearly loved each other. She couldn't imagine the grief of losing a spouse like that. Her heart contracted, and she hated herself for feeling like this for him.

Torn between sympathy and anger, Joy didn't know how to feel about Adam anymore. She couldn't like the guy, and she didn't want anything to do with him, but she felt sorry for him all the same. She mourned the man he used to be before his wife had died.

She wished she hadn't kissed him, yet part of her couldn't regret that she had.

CHAPTER EIGHT

Adam was stewing. Stewing and drinking and feeling generally sorry for himself. He knew and he wasn't proud of it. But sometimes a person needed to sit and wallow for a bit, and then you could go back to your life and move the hell on.

He finished his third beer, sighing. Morose music played in the background of his house; the lights were dimmed. If he'd put on black eyeliner and gotten his lip pierced, he could've given one of those emo kids a run for their money. Were kids still doing that these days? Adam stared at his beer can, wondering. Grace had been friends with a self-described emo kid who'd renamed himself Lucifer back in junior high, but Adam had missed that trend. Thank God.

His beer can empty, he debated whether or not four beers in two hours was excessive. Being not in the least bit slight in stature or overall body type, he barely felt buzzed. It would take a lot more than a few beers to get him hammered. And really, he didn't want to get hammered. He just wanted to take the edge off. Stop thinking for a while.

Stop obsessing over Joy.

Joy—what an ironic name for the woman causing him anything but joy. He was equal parts still angry at her and angry at himself. He could only remember the look on her face when he accused of her basically whoring herself for a story: hurt, disgust, but mostly determination. Another small part of him was proud that she'd told him to shove it. Most women would've burst into tears. Not Joy, though. She'd do what she wanted to do and no one could stop her.

He had to admire that drive, even if it was against what he wanted her to do.

A knock sounded on the door. "Adam, open up! I know you're in there!"

He glanced at the door. Grace was here. Grace was here? His little sister didn't usually venture over to his house, preferring to see him at their parents' place. Mostly because his house was rather stark at the moment, and he had to admit, depressing. Either a wall was blank or had photos of his dead wife still hanging up. It was a bit like a memorial in this house. Adam hadn't changed a thing since Carolyn had died—not replaced the sun-bleached curtains, or removed the green gingham duvet cover, or stopped using the plates they'd gotten at their wedding.

He hauled himself off the couch, grunting. His sister had her hands on her hips, her foot tapping against the welcome mat. "Took you long enough," she said irritably as she entered.

He just grunted.

Grace plopped down onto the couch. Today, her hair was in two French braids, and she wore large, hoop earrings and a flowy skirt.

"Want a beer?" he asked.

"No, I'm good."

He shrugged. He got himself another beer, although Grace made a point to give him major side-eye as he opened the can.

"What?"

She rolled her eyes. "You're pouting."

Pouting? Men didn't *pout*. They stewed, they simmered, they pondered at length—they didn't pout.

"I'm not pouting," he said, glaring at his sister. He had the petty urge to pull on her braid like when they were kids.

"Yes, you are, and you have no right to. I talked to Joy. She basically hopes you fall off a cliff and die at this point, you know."

"Is that supposed to make me feel...badly?"

Grace sighed. "Well, you shouldn't be acting like you're the hurt party. Because you were the asshole. A huge one. A gaping asshole, in fact. I had half a mind to help Joy push you off that cliff."

Well, that's a lovely sentiment to hear from one's sister, he thought. *Did his entire family want to murder him now?*

"I'm not going to apologize for getting upset," he said in a gruff voice. He took another swig of beer, feeling his blood buzz slightly from the alcohol. "I asked her not to write about the vineyard. She's doing it anyway. It's unethical and she's a liar."

Silence fell for a moment. Adam was sure he'd made his point and that Grace would leave, but she just plucked his beer can from his hand and set it on the side table. "Dearest brother," she said. "Dearest, idiotic, arrogant brother. Joy may have lied—a white lie, really—but you could've handled it all much better than you did."

"How should I have handled it?" The words came out

harsher than he intended, but dammit, she'd taken his beer and he didn't feel like being lectured by his younger sister.

"Like—I don't know—a gentleman? A thoughtful human being? You implied she was a whore and wanted to use you for her own gain. When she only wanted to help." Grace sighed again. "I get why you're touchy about it. I do. But being a complete asshole isn't going to help your case either. You might also tell her why, exactly, you're so touchy."

He stubbornly pushed away Grace's words, although they clawed at his gut regardless. He had been an asshole. He had overreacted. He had treated Joy terribly. But at the thought of telling her exactly why he had this intense antipathy toward journalists? No. He couldn't.

"I wasn't going to say this," Grace said, "but if you think Joy wasn't hurt by your words, you're wrong. I don't think she's the type who would ever show it. She'll just make your life hell in revenge. But if you'd seen her face when I talked to her? She didn't deserve that, Adam."

And now his gut was in ribbons. He had assumed— wrongly—that Joy had just been mad and would do what she wanted. But he realized that she was more like him than he'd known: pushing down her hurt feelings and vulnerability and giving the impression that no hurt had been caused.

Ah, damn. He'd fucked up majorly.

Guilt filled him until he got up and snagged his beer back. He needed something to dull that feeling. Anger he could deal with; anger meant no action was needed. But guilt? Guilt implied making things right and apologizing. Guilt implied that he'd experience its sharp hooks for years to come, tearing his skin ragged each time.

"Shit," he said before finishing off his beer.

Grace laughed, rolling her eyes again. "I'm assuming that means you're going to go beg Joy for forgiveness and then announce that you're an asshole in the town square?"

"We don't have a town square."

She waved a hand. "You know what I mean. You could do it at Trudy's. Just stand up and tell the patrons how much of a huge dick you are."

He frowned. "I thought I was just an asshole."

"Same difference. Point being, what are you going to do about it?"

He squirmed. He felt a bit like when his mom had chastised him back in grade school. *How are you going to make this right, Adam?* she'd ask him, a delicately plucked eyebrow raised.

He finally gave in and, reaching over, tugged on one of Grace's braids. "You aren't my mother, brat."

"Somebody's gotta tell you when you're screwing up," she replied with a sniff. "And Mom's too busy right now. So I'll sacrifice my time to do it."

"Wow, what a martyr you are."

She sat primly, her nose in the air, and Adam couldn't help but laugh. She smiled, laughing with him. Then she got out her phone and began texting.

His stomach roiled. "Who are you texting?"

"Joy."

"Why are you texting her?"

"To tell her you're coming by to apologize—"

He snagged the phone out of her hand, but it was too late. He heard the swoosh sound that the message had been sent. He glared at her, but she just shrugged.

"You can either sit here and pout, or do something. And now you will." She patted his shoulder. "You're welcome."

If he could strangle his sister, Adam would. Instead, he just glared at her. He was going to apologize, but in his own time. Plus, it was nine o'clock Did Joy even want people over this late?

Grace's phone sounded, and she smiled widely. "Joy says, 'I'll only forgive him if he brings strawberry macarons and white wine. And only if he begs me on his knees.' That sounds doable."

Adam didn't even know what macarons were, let alone where he'd get them. "She'll have to make do with just an apology," he said dryly.

Grace texted his response, and then laughed at her phone a few moments later. But all she said was, "Okay, she's expecting you within the hour. Get ready."

He didn't know what the hell he'd say—could he just go with a straightforward "I'm sorry" and leave it at that?—but he couldn't really get out of this, either. His sister had always been devious, but this took the cake.

Wanting to turn the tables, he swung his feet up on the nearby ottoman and said lightly, "How's Jaime?"

A blush crawled up her cheeks instantly. His sister was many things, but stoic about her crush on his executive chef and friend? Never.

"He's fine, I'm assuming," she said, looking anywhere but at Adam. "Why are you asking me?"

He snorted. "Are we really going to play this game?"

"I have no idea what you're talking about, and it's late. I need to go home." Grace stood up, almost leaving her phone. She turned and grabbed it before she got to the front door.

"You know, Jaime's single. You could always ask him out yourself instead of waiting for him."

Grace froze, her hand on the doorknob. Seeing her stiff posture, Adam felt guilty again, teasing her like this. Her crush on Jaime Martínez was a secret everyone knew. But he didn't have to tease her about, either.

Her voice was tight when she said, "It doesn't matter. He's never seen me as anything but your little sister."

Before Adam could reply, she opened the door, stepping out into the night. He'd known she had a crush on Jaime, but the pain in her voice surprised him. Was it more than that? More than a young girl's crush? And then he felt instantly stupid, because Grace wasn't a teenager anymore. She was a grown woman with a grown woman's feelings. And he'd teased her like her feelings weren't more than skin deep.

He tipped his head back and sighed. That was another apology he'd have to give. Maybe when he was eighty-five and retired he'd be able to stop insulting every woman he came into contact with.

WHEN ADAM GOT to Joy's door, it was almost ten o'clock. The sun had since set, and Mike had closed down the store hours ago. The town was deserted—no one stayed out past sunset anyway—and he felt a little like a stalker coming to her at this hour. Even though she was expecting him, and he hadn't exactly invited himself over in the first place. His fist against the door, he hesitated. Maybe he could do this tomorrow? Tell her he had an early morning tomorrow and that his little sister was a brat for texting her?

That was when the door swung open, and Joy stared at him with a mixture of amusement and annoyance.

He cleared his throat. "Hello," he said lamely.

Dressed in tiny pink pajama shorts and a gray tank, her purple hair pushed back with a headband, Joy looked like she'd been about to go to bed. At the thought of bed and Joy, Adam almost groaned. Just because he wanted to shake her until her teeth rattled didn't mean he didn't also want to kiss her. Again. And again. All over, in fact.

"How did you know I was here?" he then asked, when she just stood there.

"Anyone with half an ear could hear your tromping up those stairs. Do you have bricks attached to your boots?"

He glanced down at his sturdy boots, sans bricks. "I was just walking."

"You probably caused things to fall off the shelves in the store downstairs." When he just looked at her, she sighed. "Fine, come in. If you must."

Joy shut the door behind him, walking toward the kitchen. If Adam were a better person, he wouldn't stare at her pert little ass as she walked. He wouldn't think about how she'd moaned in her throat as he'd kissed her. So instead, he set the bottle of white wine on the counter and began looking for glasses.

"I don't know what the hell macaroons or Macarena's or whatever are," he said as he pulled out his always-at-the-ready bottle opener to uncork the wine, "but I did bring white wine. Like you asked."

She blinked, but said nothing.

He shifted on his feet. She'd asked for wine, so he'd brought it. He did own a vineyard, so he had a steady supply of the stuff. "Do you have wine glasses?"

As if coming out of a daze, she said, "Oh, yeah. Right behind you, in the left cabinet."

After pouring them both a glass, he drank the Pinot Grigio —dry, slightly fruity, one of their better bottles within the last few years—and gazed at Joy over his glass. How did a guy go about apologizing without making things worse? He had a tendency to rile this woman more than anything, no matter what he did or said.

"This is really good." She swirled the wine, smelling it. "I was kidding about the wine, but now I'm glad you took me seriously."

"I'm always serious about wine."

She looked at him, wrinkled her forehead. And then she laughed. "Was that a joke? Or at least an attempt at one? I didn't think you had it in you."

"I'm a man of many layers."

"Clearly." She continued sipping her wine, watching him.

Adam hoped that them bantering again meant she'd already forgiven him, and the cowardly part of him would've rather said nothing and left it all stuffed under the metaphorical rug. But he wasn't a kid anymore, hoping the bad things would just disappear. He set his glass down on the counter.

"Look, I wasn't planning on coming over here, but since I'm here, I should apologize." When she just waited, he had to restrain himself from squirming. "I shouldn't have talked to you like that. It was unjust and uncalled for, and I apologize."

He knew he sounded stiff, but talking about how he screwed up wasn't his strong suit. He then watched as her throat moved as she swallowed her wine. His skin prickled at the movement: it was such a subtle, yet oddly alluring movement. Or maybe he was merely fascinated with how smooth her throat and neck looked. He wanted to stroke his fingers down the slope to her shoulder, kiss her collarbone.

"I'm not going to say that I'm not still mad at you, because you were an ass to me. But I appreciate your apology nonetheless." She sipped her wine.

He rocked back on his heels. "So you forgive me, or?"

"An apology given doesn't necessitate automatic forgiveness from the wronged party," she replied, as if reciting a line from a book. "But I'll get there. The best way you can show you're sorry is to change your behavior."

He couldn't help it: he smiled wryly. She was such a spitfire that he couldn't tell if he wanted to kiss or shake her more. Maybe both at the same time.

"You always this honest when people apologize?"

"I'm always honest, all the time, with all people." She grinned widely, showing straight white teeth. "But don't think an apology doesn't go a long way to getting back on my good side."

"Well, I'm glad I haven't totally wasted my time here."

They gazed at each other, the kitchen island between them. Adam had missed this—this bantering with Joy. They hadn't known each other for long, but she brought something out in him. Whether it ended up being a good or bad thing was yet to be seen. He was also honest enough with himself to know that he was extremely attracted to her and wanted her in his bed, while another part of him remained convinced he wasn't ready for another relationship. Not after Carolyn had died so tragically, and then everything that had happened afterward.

Joy was so different from Carolyn that he couldn't reconcile the attraction to her. Then again, maybe that was why it had happened in the first place. Joy was colorful where Carolyn had been neutral; sharp and forthright where Carolyn had been diplomatic and kind. But Joy had her own beauty and intelligence and wit that made him want to know more about her. Why had she come to Heron's Landing in the first place? Who were her parents, where did she go to school, did she prefer dogs or cats, was she all sweetness and light in bed, or did she prefer things hard and fast and dirty?

At that last thought, his groin tightened, and he took a sip of wine to distract himself. Unfortunately, that just added to his slight buzz from before, and he had to stop himself from reaching out to Joy and kissing her senseless.

As if detecting his mood, she set her wineglass down on the counter, stepping toward him. She was of average height, but he was tall enough that she had to tip her head back slightly to gaze up at him. Her breasts rose and fell, and when he saw that her nipples were tight buds beneath her thin tank, he bit back a groan.

"Why are you here?" she asked. Her voice, he noted, was breathy. Breathy like when he'd kissed her by the creek.

"To apologize. Which I did. Apologize, that is."

"I think you came here for other reasons, though." She touched his chest, her hand above his heart. "Did you? Come here for other reasons?"

Yes, he wanted to say. *I came here to see you. To hear your voice, see you smile, and to kiss you again. Toss you over my shoulder and fuck you until you saw stars.*

Instead, he covered her hand with his and said in a low voice, "If you want, I can show you."

He cringed inwardly—was he some cheesy romance hero

wearing a cape saying shit like that?—but her eyes brightened. She nodded an eager little nod.

That was all he needed. Tangling his hand in her hair, he bent down and kissed her.

CHAPTER NINE

W hen Grace had texted her to tell her brother was coming by, Joy had imagined slamming her door in his face and laughing maniacally at his shocked expression. Maybe after she'd tossed her water in his face, or stepped on his foot, or kicked him in the shins. Something completely immature yet wholly satisfying. Joy hadn't kicked anyone in the shins since Marcus Terrell in fifth grade, and damn if she didn't want to see the same look of shock on Adam's face as Marcus's.

But all of her plans of shin-kicking went out the window when he'd shown up, looking delicious and apologetic. He'd even brought her wine. He'd seemed to be trying, and damn if she wasn't easy for a man who tried to right his wrongs. Maybe that made her weak.

As Adam kissed her, though, Joy couldn't find it in herself to care.

He kissed her like a man in a desert who just found an oasis, a man desperate for companionship, a man who wanted her more than any man had ever wanted her in the history of the universe. Joy had kissed a number of men—some good, some bad, some great—but this? This couldn't really compare. It was even better than that kiss down at the creek. This one wanted to strip her bare and force her soul out of her body.

It was, in a word, terrifying.

Adam tasted like wine and he kissed like a fiend. His hand cupped her ass and kneaded it with his giant hands, and Joy shivered. Her hand was still pressed against his chest, and she felt his heart pounding underneath her palm.

Suddenly, he picked her up and set her on the kitchen counter, knocking her legs apart and standing between them. Only her thin pajama shorts and his jeans kept them apart, and she could feel his erection pressing against her.

"That's better," he murmured. "I was getting a crick in my neck."

She smiled as he kissed down her throat. "We wouldn't want that."

"No, because I plan on kissing you for a long time."

Joy had to admit it—she was a kiss whore. She loved being kissed and loved kissing. Some men enjoyed it, while others did it because they knew they had to before they could get anything else. Jeremy had often gotten impatient with Joy's love of make-out sessions, while she always wondered what the damn hurry was.

But Adam? He took his time. God, he did. Tipping her head to the side, Joy sighed in absolute bliss at the feeling of his lips sliding down her neck. His beard stubble scraped the delicate skin; his teeth nipped the curve between her neck and shoulder.

"I've wanted to kiss you again since that night at the creek," he admitted. His hand moved up her tank top, caressing the small of her back. "I couldn't stop thinking about you."

The words seemed almost like a confession forced out of him, like he'd wanted to stop thinking about her but by God, he hadn't had a choice. This man, who loved being in control —what did it do to him to desire a woman who drove him crazy? Joy smiled a little at the confession. She had to admit, she loved that she made him ache. He deserved it, considering how much she'd wanted him all these weeks.

Adam slowly lowered the strap of her tank top, and Joy pulled her arm through. He didn't lower it further, though, but instead, kissed her shoulder, the inside of her elbow. She felt like her nerves were electric, buzzing and jumping at every caress. If he wanted to take her right now, she'd be ready. She scraped her nails through his hair, and he shuddered.

"Adam, Adam, kiss me," she said. She wouldn't think about how out of breath she sounded, or how desperate. She wiggled against him. "You're killing me."

"Good." He nipped her wrist then stood. Cupping her cheek, he kissed her, his tongue delving into her mouth. "I want you to beg me to fuck you. I want to hear you say how much you want me."

She laughed; he bit her bottom lip. "Why am I not surprised that you like to play the dom in bed?" Pulling away slightly, she pushed his cotton t-shirt up and over his head. She sighed in sheer pleasure, raking her fingers through the hair on his chest. He was well muscled, tan from the sun, and she traced a finger down the center of his abdomen.

That was when Joy realized he had a small tattoo on his left pectoral. Squinting, she saw that the black blob was actually a...rose? "Mr. Proper has a tattoo?" She traced the ink, looking up at him. "Who would've thought?"

"It was a long time ago. When I was dumb and young."

"Well, now you gotta tell me about it."

He took her hand away from the tattoo, and, in one swift movement, pulled her tank top over her head. "Later."

Then he bent her backward over his arm, taking a nipple into his mouth.

Joy moaned, long and low. He licked at the nipple, swirling it around in his mouth. His mouth—hot and relentless—played with her until her hips bucked against him.

"Fuck, Adam," she said on a sigh. "Your mouth should be criminal."

He bit her nipple in punishment, and she let out a yelp. But the bite of pain only intensified the pleasure as he sucked her into his mouth. He then moved to her other breast, and Joy's body prickled at seeing the nipple, red and wet with his attentions.

"You're so sweet," he muttered against her breast. "I want to lick you all over, taste every inch of you."

"Oh God, please do."

He laughed low in his throat.

If Adam Danvers were anything, it was a man who kept his promises. He kissed her belly, swirling his tongue in her belly button, and spanned her waist with his hands, stroking the sensitive skin there. She wiggled a bit, ticklish. Normally she was a bit self-conscious about the slight curve of her belly, but as Adam nipped and licked and kissed her? She didn't care. She was awash in pleasure, completely unconcerned with how she looked.

She barely noticed he had his hands hooked into the

elastic of her pink pajama shorts before she felt the cool rush of air as he pulled them off. They were going to go there, were they? Joy laid back on her elbows and watched as Adam watched her. His eyebrows rose as he kneeled, but then he stood back up again. He picked her up, and she yelped.

With little ceremony, he carried her into her bedroom and tossed her onto the bed. Pulling her toward him as he kneeled on the floor, he murmured, "Much better."

Joy had to agree. The counter sounded sexy, but really, her butt had been starting to hurt.

"Hey, as long as you're comfortable," she said prosaically. And then she yelped again when he bit the inside of her right thigh. "What is it with you and biting?"

"If you'd hush, I wouldn't have to."

"Oh, it's my fault? Typical man. Always blame—ooooh my God."

He kissed her on her mound, and she could feel the heat of his tongue against the cotton of her underwear. She knew she was wet already, and her body buzzed and her limbs shifted against the bed sheets. Her entire world focused on his mouth on her. She pushed against him, but he pushed her back down again.

"Patience," he said.

Joy moaned and groaned. She had half a mind to kick him, but as he peeled back her underwear, she forgot all about injuring him. The feeling of his fingers parting her, the cool air brushing against her folds, and the heat of his breath coalesced until she could only work toward release. Her heart pounded and her sex pounded in time with her heart, her blood heating. She knew she was flushed all over, and she didn't even care.

Then he licked her.

"Ah, I knew you'd be just as sweet down here."

She made a noise that was part moan, part squeal. She'd be embarrassed, but she was too far-gone to care now.

Her previously whining libido? It was singing with joy now.

He licked through her folds, tracing them with the tip of his tongue. Teasing her into a frenzy. Did he have to take his sweet time? She lifted her legs and set them on his shoulders, digging her heels in, an unspoken command.

But Adam wasn't one to listen, and he enjoyed her, licking and lightly sucking. Joy threw an arm over her eyes, her hips lifting in supplication. She was so close already, so close, if he'd just move…up…slightly…

That was when she felt him push a finger inside her, slowly thrusting in and out of her body. Her breathing increased.

"Joy, look at me," Adam commanded.

She moved her arm away, her eyes opening. She looked down as he fucked her with his fingers, his eyes dark, a slight flush on his cheeks. The sight of his finger disappearing inside of her, his tongue licking her and laving her? She had half a mind to burst into tears. What was he doing to her?

"Adam, Adam, Adam." She chanted his name like a prayer. She dug her heels harder into his shoulders, probably bruising him. He inserted a second finger, and then finally placed his mouth on her quivering clit. Her entire body jolted. He sucked, curving his fingers at an angle, and it only took a few more thrusts for her body to dive into complete and utter bliss.

"Fuck, fuck, fuck, Jesus Christ." Joy didn't even know what

she was saying anymore. But when he sucked her clit one last time, her body erupted, her orgasm filling every inch of her body. Her legs shuddered and a cry fell from her lips and he kept sucking and thrusting and driving her insane, the orgasm lengthening until it was almost painful.

She didn't know how much time passed. She lost herself in the pleasure, the orgasm dancing throughout her body. She bucked against his mouth and the hand on her hip. She felt wetness on her thighs and she didn't care if she were sweaty and flushed. Adam had taken her somewhere she'd never gone before, and Jesus Christ, she almost felt like getting down on her knees and thanking the good Lord for this experience.

He kissed her mound one last time before hoisting himself up, lying down beside her. She gazed at him, and he looked at her, and it was such a strange, terrifying thing that Joy couldn't —wouldn't—comprehend it. So she kissed him, tasted herself on his mouth, and wondered how this man had gotten under her skin so quickly and without her even putting up a fight.

Some moments later, Joy felt a blanket wrapping around her. Warm, soft, and comforting, she snuggled deeper into Adam's embrace. Her body was so heavy and languid, she couldn't stop her eyelids from fluttering and falling into the deepest sleep she'd had in a long time.

WHEN JOY AWAKENED to her phone dinging the following morning, she thought two things: one, why was she naked? and two: why did she feel like human putty?

Then she remembered: Adam. Adam, kissing, licking,

going down on her, and then...leaving? She rubbed her eyes and looked at the time: nine o'clock. When had he left? And why did she feel irritated that he had? They were two consenting adults and there was no shame with having fantastic oral sex and then falling asleep.

Well, she'd received fantastic oral sex. To her mortification, she'd fallen asleep without even trying to reciprocate. Not that she'd *had* to, but, common courtesy dictated that she at least say thank you.

Her phone sounded again. "Yeah, yeah, I'm coming." Then she laughed—haha, she sure had come last night! Now she was delirious. She needed some coffee.

And when she picked up her phone and saw who was texting her? Definitely coffee first. Preferably spiked with something.

Joy filled up the pot with water and dumped it in, hardly caring if she ground up enough coffee beans. She was here for the caffeine, not the taste. Plus, you couldn't get anything better than Folgers here in Heron's Landing, so acting snobby about coffee was, in a word, pointless.

Sipping the hot, vaguely coffee-tasting brew, she stared at her phone.

Can we talk? the message from Jeremy read.

I don't know, Jeremy, can we? she thought acerbically. What in the ever-loving hell did her ex want now? Couldn't she move on without him haunting her every move?

Replying, she wrote, *What is there to talk about?*

Nothing. Then the three dots. Then...her phone rang.

She stared at it. Was he really calling her? At nine thirty? She considered letting it go to voicemail, but she also knew he wouldn't let up until he got what he wanted. Better pull the bandage off and get it over with.

"Hello?" she answered. Her tone was neither chipper nor particularly sharp. She had other things on her mind more pressing than Jeremy's needy bullshit.

"Oh good, you picked up. How are you?"

Despite everything—despite his betrayal, and the fighting, and the end of something she thought had been real—her heart contracted at his voice. She hadn't heard it for weeks. Months, really. She'd loved his voice, once upon a time: cheery, amusing, always having something to tell her. She'd loved how he'd said her name, too. *Jooooy*, he'd said, elongating it. Or the nickname he'd given her, Jo-Jo.

Now though, his voice hurt. But it was a faint sting, like one that had faded and only reminded her of its presence occasionally. Not like the pain of the initial breakup.

"I'm good. Why are you calling me?"

He laughed. "Did I wake you? Sorry. I just wanted to see how things were down in Stork's Landing."

"Heron's Landing. And they're fine. How's Chicago?"

"Gorgeous, now that it's summer. But now it's gotten hot, so you picked a good time to leave. So what have you been up to down there? Still writing?"

Joy didn't know how to respond to this...banal questioning. Were they really going to act like they had no history? That Jeremy hadn't cheated on her with her best friend? Like they were cousins who chatted a few times a year about nothing because they had to?

"Yep, still writing. I'm doing a few projects for some of my Chicago clients, and some work here in Heron's Landing. Nothing extremely exciting."

She sipped her coffee, wondering how long she'd have to go through the motions. Part of her wanted to ask why Jeremy even cared, but her mind was still too languid from last night. She shivered, her body heating from the mere memory. What Adam could do with his hands and mouth should be illegal.

Jeremy took that response as a sign to tell her all about what he was doing, which she didn't really give a shit about now. Had he always been this self-centered? Probably. She just hadn't noticed until that selfishness had been turned on her. He was working primarily for a news agency in Chicago, and was hoping for a promotion soon. The money was just flooding in, he said in a cheerful voice. Joy merely stared at her apartment wall, wondering if she could act like her phone was dying to end this before she killed herself.

"But what kind of projects are you doing?" Jeremy asked her. "Is anything happening in that Podunk little town?" He laughed.

She wished she could give someone the bird through the phone. "I am working on a piece about the vineyard here. Well, trying to. The owner wasn't really into me doing it, but... You know me." She didn't even know what she was saying— just anything to end this conversation.

Jeremy asked a few more questions, and then, finally, he told her he had to go. Joy hung up with a "Thank God" before going to the living room to watch morning television. She had work to get done, but her mind couldn't concentrate on anything.

It was strange, she thought, having Adam and Jeremy collide in this way. To have Adam come over and kiss her and give her the best orgasm of her life, and then to have Jeremy talk to her like they were still engaged and he wanted to know how she felt about the day-to-day things that couples talked about. Her heart hurt for some odd reason, like she couldn't figure out how to feel. She didn't regret what she'd done with Adam, but she also felt a smidgen of fear for letting him to get close to her like this. For letting another man see her vulnerable and aching and pleading. It was easier, she'd thought, to not let anyone get close to her again after Jeremy. But that wasn't how life worked, was it?

She sipped her coffee, her thoughts tangled. She remembered the look on Adam's face as he'd touched her. And she wondered if she could expose her heart to him—or if she'd only be filled with regret instead.

CHAPTER TEN

When Adam woke up just before dawn the following morning, it took him only a nanosecond to realize where he was and what had happened only hours earlier. Plus, the light snoring coming from the woman next to him happened to be a fairly large clue.

Turning over, he gazed at Joy as she slept on, her bright purple hair rumpled and her cheeks flushed with sleep. Her face, softened in repose, made his heart contract in a way he didn't want to examine too closely. He brushed the hair from her forehead and kissed her in the spot between her eyebrows before getting up. At first he'd considered waking her, but she seemed so at peace that he hated to force her out of her deep sleep.

Not to mention, he didn't know what he would do if she woke up and smiled at him like she had last night. She had become a bigger weakness than he could've ever imagined. But what could come of their relationship? The ghost of his wife haunted him, and he had a difficult time seeing Joy happy in a place like Heron's Landing for long. He knew she was running from something—someone—and once she figured things out, she'd bolt for brighter, busier places. While he'd stay here, tending the failing vineyard, and wondering if the blood, sweat and tears he put into those vines would ever yield fruit.

He drove home and took a quick shower and changed. He had to be at River's Bend in a couple of hours to begin events planning, and he needed to be as focused as possible. He couldn't be seen mooning over a woman. Going to the kitchen, he stopped and gazed at a photo of Carolyn, one taken only a few months before the accident. He picked up the frame, stroking her face. *What am I doing?* he asked her—asked himself. *What should I do, Caro?*

Carolyn only smiled back, her eyes creased with happiness. Adam had taken the photo himself, and it'd been the day his dad had given over River's Bend to him officially, three years prior. He and Carolyn had been so elated that day. She'd also looked so beautiful amongst the crop that he took some photos of her in the sunlight, smiling and beaming.

But those days were long past, even though they didn't seem like that long ago. Carolyn was gone, the vineyard was failing, and he had slept with—almost slept with, he supposed —another woman who was simultaneously a thorn in his side and a beacon in the darkness.

Arriving at the vineyard, Jaime drove up about the same time as he did. Getting out of his red SUV, Jaime muttered good morning as he made his way inside to begin planning for the day's menu. Adam's chef had never been a morning person, preferring to wake up after the sun had long arisen and working well into the night. But that didn't work with River's Bend's schedule; thus, he got to work cranky and tired for a few hours before he perked up and was his usual, charming, sarcastic self.

Seeing Jaime made Adam think of his remarks to Grace, and he winced. What had gotten into him, to mess with his younger sister's emotions like that? He knew he'd wanted to deflect his problems and move them onto her. That didn't make it fair or right, and he knew he owed her a real apology. He also wondered if Grace would ever act on her infatuation, or would she stand in the shadows, longing but never touching? Adam shook his head. For one, his sister's love life was not anything he wanted to think about, and two, he had much bigger problems to tackle. Grace was a big girl; she could handle herself.

The entire team got together—Jaime, Leah, Kerry, and Chris—and began a strategy for planning their first event. Kerry had already put together various social media pages, not yet launched, while Leah had actually put out feelers for anyone potentially interested in doing events at the vineyard. "We'd be better off starting with someone local," Leah said in her usual flat tones. "Someone who doesn't expect bells and whistles."

Adam would've rather gone outside the community, as Heron's Landing was too insular to begin with, but it was a start. Leah gave him some names, including Sadie Parsons and Tanya Eckhart, both recently engaged and looking around for potential wedding venues. Adam knew Sadie somewhat, as she'd gone to school with Grace, while he had only met Tanya a few times, as she'd moved out of town after high school before returning recently. Both, he knew, were good, country kinds of girls. But would they even have the funds to pay what River's Bend would need to be successful?

Tension roiled in Adam's gut, and a headache threatened to build in his temples.

He also knew that he had to reach out to potential candidates himself. Calling both Sadie and Tanya, he spoke to them about their ideas regarding their weddings and their interest in doing it at River's Bend. Both were excited and happy to talk all day about their weddings and their fiancés, and their happiness couldn't help but rub off on Adam somewhat. By the end of the day, he felt more optimistic about the entire venture—and couldn't wait to talk to Joy about it, either.

As Adam was about to leave, though, he saw Jaime staring at his phone, his brow furrowed.

"Bad news?" Adam asked.

Jaime glanced up, and then shook his head. "No, just... frustrating news. You know my parents are working on becoming citizens? Well, there's always some other fee to pay, some other hoop to jump through." He rubbed his forehead. "Too bad I'm just a chef, not a lawyer."

"Any way I can help?"

Jaime smiled a little. "Not really, but thanks for the offer. I won't torture you with all of this paperwork, anyway."

Adam knew Jaime's parents' situation weighed on him. His father worked as a professor of biochemistry at the University of Iowa, while his mom had run her own small retail business for decades. They'd emigrated from El Salvador before Jaime had been born, luckily able to come to the United States legally with the university sponsoring Jaime's father for a work visa.

But that didn't mean becoming citizens was any easier, and it had been such an arduous, lengthy process that Adam couldn't imagine how stressful it had been for the entire Martínez family.

As the two men were about to get into their separate cars, another car showed up and parked. Adam watched as Grace stepped out, a bag in hand, humming underneath her breath. When she saw Adam, she waved; when she saw, Jaime, she froze and looked so much like a deer in headlights that Adam wanted to take her home and give her a drink.

"Adam, Jaime," she said, glancing at Jaime but focusing solely on Adam. "I was just dropping off Kerry's sweater. She left it at my place this weekend, and the vineyard's closer than her house, so…"

Grace was so pointedly ignoring Jaime that Adam winced inwardly, but he only said, "She's just inside."

"Okay, great. I was afraid I was going to miss her. Thanks." She turned, blushing, and said, "How are you, Jaime?"

Jaime had been looking off into the distance, and it took him a second to realize Grace was speaking to him. "Oh, fine. You still painting?"

She nodded, her chin tucked into her chest. She clutched her bag to her stomach like a shield.

When she still said nothing, Jaime just raised a dark eyebrow and said, "Well, I gotta go." He chucked Grace under the chin. "You be good, huh, kid?"

The sound of Jaime driving off was the only one for a moment as Grace and Adam stood next to each other. Adam heard Grace's breath hiccup, and he was terrified she'd start crying.

"That was so bad," she whispered.

"It wasn't…not really." He was lying—so he stopped talking.

"He sees me as a little kid. Oh God, and I act like one too!" She whirled on Adam, saying in a harsh whisper, "Do not tell anyone about this, you got it? No. One." She stalked into the building behind them, Adam at a loss for words.

He hated seeing his sister unhappy, but he also couldn't encourage a romance between her and his employee. He rubbed his temples. Maybe Joy would know how to handle this. At the thought of her, he perked up—in more places than one.

If he drove faster than usual as a result to get to her place, he would never, ever admit it.

"So how was work today?" Joy asked as she poured Adam a glass of wine from the bottle he'd brought over yesterday. She seemed in good spirits, smiling as she opened the door for him and even kissing him before he entered. He'd taken that as a good sign, and they may have kissed in the doorway longer than necessary.

"We're going forward with the events. I still don't love the idea, but it's pretty much all we have right now." He swirled the wine, inhaling its notes before sipping it. "I even talked to potential brides."

Joy raised her eyebrows. "You did? You didn't make them cry, did you?"

"No, they were very happy to consider my services."

"Look at you, charming women left and right. Next you'll be blogging about weddings and talking about the best dresses for the season."

"There are seasons for dresses?" At her look, he grinned.

He couldn't help it: she brought something out in him that no one had in a long time. Even Carolyn. Reaching for Joy, he took her into his arms, nuzzling her neck. She smelled heavenly, and had the softest skin. "Are you wearing perfume?" he asked, curious suddenly.

"Mmmm, yes. I bought a new kind before I left Chicago—Chloé by Chloé. Very original, no?"

"You smell like flowers." He inhaled. He'd been trained to detect subtle notes of fragrance in wines, and found himself able to do so similarly for perfumes. "I smell rose, maybe a layer of cedarwood? And amber."

She looked up at him, her eyes wide. "How did you—? That's impressive. I think there's also honey and peony, if I remember correctly."

He kissed up her throat, no longer caring about the various notes of the perfume. "You also taste like sugar."

"That's probably the Dial soap I bought from Mike's."

When he pinched her, she giggled.

Although he could've taken her on the counter right then —just like last night—he backed away. Brushing her hair behind her ear, he asked, "How long did you live in Chicago?"

Her expression became shuttered. She looked away, suddenly invested in the plate of crackers she'd set out. "For about seven years," she finally said. "I grew up in Springfield, Illinois, as a kid but moved to Chicago after college."

"And you were a journalist in Chicago, too?"

"Freelance writer, journalist, barista, dog walker, you name it, I did it. When you're young, you think the world's your oyster and that even if a city is expensive, you'll figure it out." She smiled a little. "I was poor, but happy. I think that's the best part of your twenties, you know? Figuring out shit and doing whatever, never knowing what the next day will bring."

Adam couldn't really agree, as he'd known since he was a kid that he'd take over River's Bend and run the family business. He'd also known he'd marry a good woman like Carolyn, stay in Heron's Landing, and have a few kids. The usual kind of thing—just like his father. But now Carolyn was gone, he had no children, and the vineyard was failing as he stood here with Joy in his arms. Maybe if he'd been as free as Joy had been in her early twenties, he wouldn't feel so at sea when things hadn't gone exactly as planned.

"And then I met Jeremy," she continued, "and I thought we'd stay in Chicago forever. But that didn't happen."

Adam stopped himself from asking more. Grace had mentioned that Joy had had a boyfriend—fiancé?—but Adam knew nothing more than that. He wondered if this Jeremy had something to do with her moving away from Chicago to a tiny town like Heron's Landing. Gently, he asked, "What happened after that?"

She shrugged, but he could see the tension in her face. "Things didn't work out, I guess. And now here I am." She tried to smile, but he could tell this wasn't something she wanted to talk about.

Adam touched her arm. "I'm sorry."

"It's over and done with." She sipped her wine, and then asked, "What about you? What was your wife like?"

For some reason, he hadn't expected her to ask about Carolyn. It felt so strange, talking about his wife with the woman he'd kissed and pleasured last night. Strange, yet…not. His family had a tendency to avoid the subject of Carolyn, and he found himself wanting to talk about her. She'd always be part of his life; acting like she hadn't existed wouldn't make his grief over her death disappear.

"Carolyn was one of those people who everyone liked. Kind, funny, generous. She was about your height, but with blond hair."

Joy smiled. "Where did you meet?"

"In college. We took a business class together, and I sat behind her. She said no to me twice before she agreed to go out with me. She wore a blue sweater and her hair in a bun on our first date. I'll never forget it."

The moment turned silent, but not awkwardly. Sadness filled him, but also, an odd sense of, well, joy. He'd been lucky to know and love Carolyn, and although he'd always miss her, she was gone. The first months after Carolyn's death had been a haze of grief and anger. Adam could barely remember those months. As time passed, though, the haziness of the grief had transformed into a day-to-day sadness, an ache that would never go away. The smallest things broke his heart—eating her favorite dish, watching a TV show she liked—and sometimes he didn't know if he could go on.

But time had gone on. The grief would always exist, no matter how many years passed. Adam also knew that he'd never be the same person as before, but he'd be okay. He'd survive.

Now, though, he stood with this woman, a woman who was very present and alive and beautiful in her own right. Her bright hair, and bright eyes, the freckles scattered across her face, her nails painted a bright red, and even the strap of her blue bra coalesced to make her seem like a fanciful creature, too lovely for mere mortals to gaze upon. He wanted to trace the lovely angle of her collarbones, kiss the inside of her elbows, tease the skin of her slim ankles.

"You remind me of a fairy," he found himself saying.

She laughed, caught off guard. "A fairy? Do I have wings sprouting behind me?"

"No, but you're a creature who's hard to catch and harder to find. And you're all colors and light." He brushed her cheek with his thumb.

Her chest rose, pushing her breasts up, and he had the urge to bury his face there. Lick her and taste her and inhale every inch of her. "I never knew you were so fanciful," she murmured.

"Only with you."

He kissed her, setting his wine glass on the counter behind her. She didn't taste like a fairy, though: she tasted of woman, flesh and blood and heat and silk. After stripping off his t-shirt and hers, he backed her into her bedroom. They fell onto the bed in a tangle of limbs, and he hardly knew where he began and she ended. His thumbs brushed her hipbones; she shimmied underneath him, her breath fanning his cheek.

That was when she unzipped his jeans and, taking his hardened cock into her hand, he tipped his head back and groaned. He watched her pale, slim fingers encircle his cock, which grew larger at her ministrations. She stroked him, at once tightly and like a butterfly's wing, and it was absolute torment.

She moaned a little underneath her breath. "I had a feeling you were packing, but you, sir, exceeded my expectations."

"I'm glad not to disappoint."

She smiled widely, climbing on top of him, letting go of his cock. He almost protested, but then he forgot about it when she smiled, her teeth flashing, as she unclasped her bra and let it fall down her arms. She tossed it behind her before cupping one breast. He watched, enthralled, as she played with her breasts, tweaking a nipple and moaning as she did it. His cock bobbed in front of her, and he almost tipped her over to take over.

"Jesus Christ, Joy," he ground out. "Let a man live, will you?"

She took his hand, placing it over her pounding heart. He stroked down her sternum, his fingers brushing the underside of one breast. Softness, heat, pale skin. It was straight out of a fantasy, this fairy woman playing with herself on top of him.

She then moved down and, her face level with his groin, licked the length of his cock. He bucked, pleasure piercing through his limbs. If she weren't careful, he'd come just from her light touch.

Joy swirled her tongue around the head, sucking him briefly. He cursed; she grinned. She continued licking and sucking and when she fondled him, too, he could feel his balls drawing up into orgasm.

He tipped her over onto the bed, looming over her. "Playtime's over," he said.

He pulled off her shorts and underwear while she reached into her bedside drawer for a condom. She ripped it open and rolled the latex down his cock. He kissed her, their tongues tangling. He parted her folds, and he groaned at how wet she was. He knew she deserved a lengthy seduction, but it'd been too long. He hadn't had sex since his wife died, and the desperation filling him couldn't be ignored. And as Joy lifted her hips against him, saying his name, he knew she was as desperate as he was.

He positioned his cock at her entrance and pushed inside. Stars burst behind his eyelids, and Joy gripped his shoulders. A bead of sweat rolled down his face, and when she reached up and licked it, he shuddered.

Adam thought to wait for her to adjust, but he couldn't. At Joy's small cry as he thrust out and slammed back into her, she couldn't wait either. His rhythm was jerky, frantic, but Joy just wrapped her arms around his neck and held on. She worked herself on his cock, and they chased their mutual pleasure. He bit her shoulder, and her nails dug into his shoulders.

"So wet, so tight," he muttered, not even knowing what he was saying at this point as he thrust inside her. "You drive me crazy."

She laughed a little, but then moaned as he brushed against her clit. "Don't stop. Don't you dare stop. I'm so close."

Words were lost at this point. They kissed and their teeth clashed and it was eager and messy, and the bed hit the wall in time to their rhythm. Adam felt his orgasm coiling, a spring about to release, and he lifted Joy's legs for a deeper angle.

Her eyes widened as he fucked her this way, and then she moaned loud and long. "Oh my God, Jesus Christ, fuck me, God!"

He grinned, making sure to keep her legs up so he could thrust against that one particular spot. Wetness coated his cock, and the sounds of their joined bodies coupled with the sound of the bed hitting the wall created the most erotic experience of Adam's life.

Joy didn't say anything more. Instead, she tipped her head back further and further, her throat exposed, and as Adam scraped his teeth along its length, she shuddered. She made a low sound. And then her body erupted: full body shivers that coalesced into her sheath contracting around him in urgent pulses.

He thrust his tongue into her mouth as she came, and then only a few moments later, he was coming, too. He swore, feeling his balls draw up and then his entire body filled with intense pleasure. He jerked inside of her, his hands gripping her legs, and it went on and on and on. So long that he felt a little dizzy as he began to come down from the high.

"Jesus Christ, Joy," he said. He collapsed next to her, trying to catch his breath.

She stretched an arm over her head, smiling slyly, languid and gorgeous in the dim light. "That was nice," she murmured.

He barked out a laugh. Nice? How about transformative? But seeing her sleepy, sly look, he pulled her close and kissed her collarbone, her ear, any place he could find. She wiggled and laughed, and then sighed.

Time seemed to come to a standstill. Adam couldn't stop touching her, even though he wanted to sleep for a week. But when Joy turned onto her stomach, her chin on her hands, he felt himself harden as he gazed at her pert little ass. Would he ever stop wanting this woman?

"I think I'm going to take a shower," she said, licking her lips. "Wanna join?"

His idea to fall asleep went straight out the window. He picked her up, tossing her over his shoulder, Joy squealing.

CHAPTER ELEVEN

J oy smiled as she finished the last paragraph of her story about River's Bend. She planned to reintroduce the subject to Adam later that day, especially now that the vineyard was expanding into events. Mostly, though, she was giddy about everything else that had happened recently: Adam, sex, kissing, Adam, sex. Lots of sex. Adam had come over every night for the past week, and each time they slept together, it was unlike anything Joy could describe.

The sex wasn't hours-long or intense, acrobatic Tantric sex that you could base a series of erotica novels off of. It didn't involve sex swings (although Joy had joked about getting one) or giant dildos or even anything other than oral and your traditional penis-vagina sex in various positions. But being so close to Adam, touching his body, his hands running down her body, the way he felt inside of her? She had a difficult time describing all of the various emotions that ran through her mind each time they had sex. And *she* was the writer.

But adjectives, verbs, nouns—they all failed her. The sex

possessed a language entirely its own, one that Joy was only learning as the days passed. Sometimes she'd see something in his gaze that caused her heart to contract, and when he curled his fingers into hers, she never wanted to let him go.

She was, she thought wryly, becoming rather maudlin in her old age.

Today, though, Joy finished this first draft of her story about the vineyard, one that featured the beginning of it doing events, and she printed off a copy before heading to her car. She could've sent Adam a copy electronically, but he was a dinosaur at heart and probably didn't like to read anything on a screen. That was something she loved about him.

Joy stilled at the thought, her hand above her car door handle. Love? Adam? L-O-V-E? She shook her head. No, she *liked* certain things about him. She *liked* the way he kissed her, and how he brought her new bottles of wine. She liked his hands and the dark hair running along his forearms. But nothing about love, not real love, not the love she thought she'd had with Jeremy.

She winced at the thought of her ex-fiancé. Jeremy had been texting her more and more lately, wanting to talk to her about...she didn't even know. What was there to say? He wouldn't apologize, yet he wouldn't leave her alone, either. It was as if the thought of her daring to leave him after he'd cheated on her flew right over his pretty, narcissistic little head. She'd considered changing her number, but part of her didn't want to admit his messaging her posed a problem. Plus, changing her number would signal to him that he was getting to her, and Joy preferred to win a battle of wills at all costs. Was it stupid? Yes. But at least she'd win.

As she pulled up at River's Bend ten minutes later, all

thoughts of her ex fled her mind. The day shone bright, with the temperature hovering at a bearable eighty-five degrees. For late July in Missouri, that was practically sweater weather. When she got out of the car, pushing her sunglasses on top of her head, she watched as Adam walked toward her.

And, because she was an idiot, her heart pounded so hard her body buzzed.

"Good morning," Adam said, bending down to kiss her. "I didn't think you got up before ten o'clock most days."

She smiled sweetly. "If I get a chance to bother you, I'll get up before the sun. It's my number one goal in life at the moment."

"How comforting. Dare I ask why you've driven here and how you're going to torment me?"

"Maybe in a bit. Get me some of that amazing coffee you make. Oh, did the pastry chef make beignets this morning?"

Adam brushed a thumb across her collarbone. "So mercenary. No beignets, but we do have donuts."

"Perfect. Lead the way to my baked goods."

She laughed when he pinched her ass, and in revenge, she promptly slapped his ass. Since when had this playful man come out? When she'd first met Adam Danvers, he'd been irritable, rude, and perpetually constipated (so Joy had assumed). Now, though, he grinned at her and pinched her on the butt like some teenage boy. What was next, a teddy bear and balloons to commemorate sleeping together for an entire week without killing each other?

Joy's phone buzzed, and pulling it out, she saw that Jeremy had texted her. Again. *Can I call you tonight?* it read. And then the kicker: winky face emoji. A winky face! The man must have balls of steel to send her a winky face.

She must've made a face, because Adam stepped up and asked in a low voice, "Something wrong?"

She jumped. "No, nothing," she said as she stuffed her phone into her purse. "Just a stupid text from a friend. So where are those donuts you promised?"

Adam peered at her, like he was going to say something, but right then Kerry bounced up to them.

"Joy! How are you? Are you here for the wine-tasting class later?"

Joy smiled, ignoring Adam's look of confusion. "Nope, just here to bug your boss. Although I'll have to do the class sometime. Anything to drink more wine, right?"

"I'll tell you a secret: Leah serves way more wine on Mondays, mostly because she hates Mondays. I've seen patrons have to be carried to their cars afterward."

"Noted." Turning to Adam, Joy said, "Be sure to sign me up for Monday's class, would you?"

He rolled his eyes. "Kerry, don't encourage her. Let's get you some coffee before you do something stupid."

As they walked away from the younger woman, Joy whispered, "Like sleep with you? Is that stupid enough?"

She had to bite her cheek to keep from laughing when he snapped the back of her bra like a middle school boy before leaning down and saying, "Watch your mouth, or I'll make you pay later."

"I can't wait."

Joy found the coffee quickly enough, and she found herself watching Jaime and his staff prepping for the day. Jaime called out stations, telling his sous chef that if he burned the duck again he'd burn *him*, and mostly Joy was surprised no one started crying. Jaime had brass balls, she realized, and she sipped her coffee, admiration filling her. She liked a guy with balls, and Jaime was as confident as any person in that kitchen.

"What are we having today, Jaime?" Adam asked, taking some donuts from a nearby counter.

"Hey, Adam. Roast duck with garlic broccolini in white wine sauce, plus raspberry tarts."

"Raspberries again?"

"Yeah, because somebody—" a glare at one of the staff "—ordered twenty pounds instead of two, and now we're trying to use them up before they go bad."

Joy couldn't help but piping up. "You know if you soak berries in vinegar for a bit, they'll last longer?"

Jaime turned to her, an eyebrow raised, as if shocked anyone would give him tips in his kitchen. Joy, though, merely smiled widely at his expression.

"You don't say?" Jaime said.

"Yep. Try it and let me know how it works for you." She snagged a donut from Adam and began munching on it. "Great donuts! See you all later."

She and Adam eventually made their way to his office, where Joy sat him down and made him tell her everything about doing events at the vineyard. He still seemed like he'd rather eat rocks than talk about weddings and bridal parties, but Joy could only be excited. She *loved* weddings. The dresses, the flowers, the invitations, the food, the shoes, the jewelry—everything. When she'd had to cancel her dress order when Jeremy cheated on her, she'd been so mad that only a large bottle of wine had stopped her from finding Jeremy and choking him out.

"We're currently in talks with two local brides," Adam explained. "They both seemed interested. We're going to start small, see how it goes, and continue from there."

Joy pulled out the story she'd written and handed it over to Adam. "I know you think journalists are Satan's minions, but I would still highly recommend allowing me to write about River's Bend. It'll be free publicity. How could you say no to that?"

She had to admit, she was still a bit nervous about his reaction. He may have apologized, but that didn't mean he was cool with the idea yet, either. As she held out the papers, he stared at them like she was handing him a dismembered arm in a box. She set them on the desk with a pat.

"Adam, have you ever considered talking to someone about your fear of free publicity?"

He glared at her, but it was tinged with amused exasperation. "Has anyone told you you're a giant pain in the ass?"

"All the time. Doesn't change the fact that I'm right."

He grunted.

Silence fell, and Joy fidgeted. "Look," she finally said. "I know you aren't super into writing about the vineyard or whatever. I don't get it, but I know it's a thing now. Just, at least think about it. Okay? Make a pros and cons list even."

He picked up the papers, glancing at them before setting them next to him. "I'll read through this. Thank you for letting me see it first."

She rolled her eyes, but couldn't help but smile, too. This exasperating man was going to be the death of her.

Her phone sounded again, and a chill went through her. And then it sounded again, and again. Message after message.

Adam looked at her, and then said, "You going to answer that?"

No, she thought. *I know who it is and he sucks monkey balls and I hope he falls off a cliff.* She gritted her teeth. "Not particularly interested in responding," she said.

"Who's texting you so much this morning?" He didn't say it with jealousy lacing his voice, necessarily, but more concern that she was potentially ignoring something important.

How did she tell her current…fling? lover? that her ex-fiancé was intent on talking with her no matter what she told him? When her phone sounded again, she pulled it out with a curse, and then swore again as she read Jeremy's texts.

"What is it?" Adam asked, concern in his voice.

Joy hesitated. But at his look, she admitted, "It's my ex. He's just being a pain in the ass. Don't worry about it." At Adam's look, she winced inwardly. For all Adam knew, she and Jeremy were still on somewhat good terms and she was playing two men at once. She almost blurted that Jeremy had cheated on her with her best friend, but then she stopped herself. The thought of telling him of such a betrayal made her want to sink into the floor. Oddly enough, Jeremy's betrayal had only been one layer of hurt: the other had been humiliation that she'd been cheated on. That she couldn't keep a boyfriend interested enough not to fuck her friend. Oh, sure, it was Jeremy's—and Regina's—decision, not Joy's, but that didn't mean it hadn't been a blow to Joy's self esteem, either.

So now she bit her tongue and gathered her things, a jumble of emotions. "I should go. Let me know what you think of the story, okay? Have a good day."

She didn't even kiss him goodbye, and she could've slapped herself. Way to be obvious that something was up, and now because she was a total coward, he was probably thinking the worst.

Is your pride important enough to let this man think badly of you? her mind whispered.

The sad thing was that Joy wasn't sure of the answer.

"You need to tell him." Grace pulled a Twizzler from the package and bit on the end.

"Easier said than done." Pointing her own Twizzler at the girl, Joy added, "You have no room to speak about being honest with a guy, missy."

Joy had invited Grace over for a girl's evening, needing someone to talk to about Adam. Well, not the details—Grace was his sister, after all—but about Jeremy and Adam and Joy's poor life choices. She'd confessed to Grace that Jeremy had cheated on her, albeit after a few drinks. But now that she and the younger girl both had secrets that they'd revealed to each other, they felt a camaraderie that was stronger than it had been initially.

"This isn't about me," Grace said prosaically. "You called me to talk about yourself. Plus, I'm working on a plan."

Joy perked up. "A plan? Tell me!"

"No, not until you tell my brother the truth."

Joy slumped down into the couch, biting off more of the Twizzler. "I'd rather guzzle gasoline," she admitted.

"You're so dramatic. It's not like you did anything wrong."

"It's not that, it's just that…" Joy looked away, her throat closing a little. "It's humiliating, you know? I hate the look people get on their faces when you tell them. Pity mixed with questions."

"Questions?"

"Yeah, like, 'how'd she fuck up so badly that her boyfriend slept with her best friend?' Those kinds of questions."

Grace rubbed Joy's knee. "Oh, Joy, I can't imagine anyone thinking that."

"My mom certainly did. Asked me point blank if I'd been withholding sex and if that's why Jeremy had strayed. That had been the low point of my life, let me tell you."

"Well, your mom can eat a moldy dick, as you would say. No one's at fault for cheating except the cheater. Even if you shaved his eyebrows while he slept and cursed his future children, he still made that shitty decision." Grace nodded, finishing her Twizzler and then sipping on some wine Adam had brought over earlier. "And I know Adam isn't going to judge *you* for it."

"I guess." Joy didn't think so, either, but that didn't make it any easier. Desperately wanting to change the subject, she asked, "Have you been painting lately?"

Grace had majored in art and had specifically worked with watercolors while in school, and Joy had gotten to see a few of her pieces. They had been surprisingly dark for a seemingly sunny girl like Grace Danvers: images of dark oceans and skies and places that made Joy shudder, faces of women shrouded in black and gray, and some pieces that couldn't be easily explained but that exuded a roiling emotion that Joy found both distressing and infinitely compelling.

Lately, though, Grace hadn't been painting much, which she'd confessed to Joy a few weeks ago. Joy had a feeling she felt a little lost after graduating and then moving back home, stuck in her parents' house while she figured out the terrifying question of what-are-you-going-to-do-with-your-life.

Grace smiled a little sadly. "I started one a few days ago, but it was awful. Just a jumble of barf colors. I threw it out."

"Maybe you need new inspiration. Perhaps a day trip somewhere new?"

"Maybe." Grace didn't sound convinced. "Maybe I need to try painting fewer landscapes. I could try more people."

Joy smiled widely. "You should hire some models. Nude models. Wonder if Jaime would be down?"

"Joy!" Grace yelled, hitting her with a pillow. "I will never ask Jaime Martínez to pose naked for me!"

"Too bad. I bet he'd be a great subject."

"You say one more word about him and I'm going to poison your drink."

"No you won't, because then who would you go see hot-guy movies with?"

Grace sniffed. "I'll go with my mom."

"How thrilling. I always love watching hunks with my mom in tow."

Grace just hit her with a pillow again.

The evening wound down, with the wine still flowing. Joy made Grace sit on the floor so she could play with her hair—perfect for braiding, as it was long and flowy—and she tried to convince the girl to continue painting. "I'm not a painter, obviously—I can't even draw a stick figure—but I think we're kind of in the same boat, since I'm a writer. You just have to push through any writer's block. Or painter's block, as it may be."

Grace sighed as Joy tugged a strand of hair into the French braid she was creating. "It's not that. It's like...I can't paint. It's as if there's nothing there."

"What's not there, hun?"

"The skills? The inspiration? I don't know. I used to paint all the time. Now, though, I take out my watercolors and it's almost painful to pick up a paintbrush." She sighed, and it was such a sad sigh that it went straight to Joy's heart. "I think I'm broken."

No, I think you're depressed, Joy thought. Instead, she rubbed the girl's shoulder. "You're not broken, just a little stuck. You'll get there, I promise. I think your twenties are more about trying not to fuck everything up than they are about becoming some accomplished adult. Believe me, you're doing as great as any twenty-three year old out there."

"What were you doing at my age?"

Joy pulled another piece of hair, biting her lip in concentration. "Writing, mostly. Eating ramen noodles. Wondering if I should be responsible and go to law school like my mom wanted. The usual early twenties' angst."

"Why didn't you go to law school?"

"Because I didn't want to. I knew it wouldn't make me happy. It's funny, people think young people are inherently selfish, but I think so much of your twenties is trying to do what other people want you to do. Trying to make others happy with your choices because you're young and don't know what you really want. But at the end of the day," she said as she finished tying off the braid, "if you're not happy, no one else will be, either."

Grace didn't say anything, but Joy saw the girl brush something off her cheek. She squeezed her shoulders, hoping deep in her heart that Grace would find that happiness she so rightly deserved.

CHAPTER TWELVE

With his feet propped up on his desk, Adam set Joy's story down, rubbing his chin. It was good—great, even. He hadn't really known what to expect of Joy's writing abilities, but she'd impressed him. She had a stylish tone that permeated her writing, and he could almost hear her voice in his ear as he'd read the article.

She'd made River's Bend sound like an up-and-coming attraction, as opposed to a declining vineyard in the middle of nowhere. She'd even described the owner as a "dedicated individual with an immense knowledge of wines," which he had to admit he'd smiled at. Thinking about the last time he'd read about himself in a story, he scowled, forcing those memories away. This was Joy, and hadn't she already shown him that she wasn't like the journalists that had almost ruined his and his family's lives? Joy may use writing to pay her bills, but she clearly respected boundaries and didn't use other people's pain and misfortune for a quick buck, either.

He was just about to text her to let her know she could publish the article when his phone rang. "This is Adam," he said when he picked up, mostly out of habit than because it was rare anyone other than him ever used his phone.

"Sadie and Robert are here for their meeting," Kerry chirped in his ear. "Should I send them back?"

Adam had completely forgotten that the couple was coming to River's Bend to discuss using it for their wedding. "I'll come get them. Be sure to offer them something to drink, if they're interested."

Ten minutes later, Adam seated the couple across from his desk, apologizing for the mass of papers and folders scattered across the surface. He rarely had meetings in his office, and certainly not with people he'd consider clients. But both Sadie Parsons and Robert Lyle had grown up in Heron's Landing, and they hardly noticed the lack of décor. Sadie was a plump, blond girl no older than twenty-two, her hair in ringlets that made her look like Goldilocks. Her fiancé, in complete contrast, was dark-headed and rather taciturn, preferring to grunt his responses and rarely using complete sentences. They were the exact opposite in terms of personalities, yet they seemed to complement each other perfectly. Adam didn't understand it, but he had to admit that they only had eyes for each other.

Sadie brought an entire binder full of ideas, pointing to flower arrangements and table setups and even aisle runners until Adam's head spun. Robert offered nothing beyond a few grunts of agreement when Sadie prompted him, although he did end up saying, "No pink, Sadie," to which his fiancée gave him a sad pout.

Adam scribbled down Sadie's jumbled ideas, his own head whirling. He had no idea what he was doing, did he? How did he think he could become some wedding coordinator and just hope things worked, when they hadn't worked the first time around? But he kept a straight face as he talked with Sadie, nodding and offering any suggestions that happened to spring to mind. By the end of the meeting, he'd gathered that the bride wanted a country wedding with loads of flowers and that she hated carrot cake. When she began talking about her dress and the cowboy boots she'd wear with it, Adam had to restrain the urge to put his head down on his desk.

He escorted them out, shaking hands with both and telling them he'd be in contact with them shortly. That was when he spotted a bright purple head out of the corner of his eye, and to his surprise, Joy was at his elbow, asking if Sadie and Robert were the bride and groom to be.

"Oh, congratulations! I love weddings. Did you two just finish talking to Adam?" Joy asked, a gleam in her eye.

Adam almost told her that the couple was headed home, but Sadie responded to Joy's enthusiasm equally. "We did. We're still considering between River's Bend or having it at Robert's parents' home."

"You have to have it at River's Bend! It'll be so gorgeous, overlooking the river as the sun sets behind you two. What does your dress look like?"

Adam hadn't seen Joy this excited since she'd discovered that she could order her favorite kind of potato chips from Chicago online. He watched her and Sadie talk animatedly, Robert simply standing aside and letting his fiancée talk. Adam had a feeling that was Robert's usual role, and the guy didn't seem the least bit discomfited by it.

"If you have the wedding here," Joy was saying, "I could write a story about it, since it would be the first one River's Bend would be hosting. I could even contact some friends of mine in Chicago, see if they want to provide some things for the wedding. You know, sponsor you and then I write about them, and they get free advertising." She snapped her fingers. "Easy as that. Plus, it would generate more revenue for me, too," she added with a wide smile.

Sadie laughed, but Adam shifted on his feet. "Once we make our decision," Sadie said, "I'll let you know. I'd love to have our wedding made into a story, though. Wouldn't that be romantic, Robbie?"

Robert grunted, and Sadie beamed.

The couple finally departed, a wide smile on Joy's face and Adam trying hard to keep his misgivings to himself. So what if Joy wanted to make some money? his logical brain told him. That didn't mean she was going to screw him and everyone else over to write some op-ed piece that could hurt people as a result. But the anxiety surrounding the subject still niggled at him, and when Joy turned to him, her smile slowly disappeared.

"Are you okay?" she asked, peering at him closely. "You look like you're going to puke."

Kerry, sitting at her desk, was watching the exchange closely, and although the town had already figured out that Adam and Joy were canoodling (Kerry's favorite word), he also didn't want to advertise their canoodling, either. Especially not if it resulted in some disagreement.

He took her aside and kissed her cheek. "Want to come over later?" he asked quietly. He didn't want to think about stories or journalists or anything else. And with Joy pressed into his side, her sweet scent filling his nose, all of his worries dissipated like mist.

Joy glanced at him, but her expression became mischievous. "Maybe, if I have time," she replied airily. "Do you have something good to give me?"

"Sweetheart, I always have something good to give you. And if you come over, I'll show you exactly what I mean." He kissed the side of her neck, a place where he knew she was extra sensitive. She shuddered a little in his arms.

But it was what she said next that made his eyes widen. "How about you take me back to your office and show me right now?"

Adam, to put it plainly, had never been that kind of guy. His life was orderly, pristine, and he made love in beds and the occasional countertop. Always at home, and never at work. Hell, he and Carolyn had been so busy they'd almost had to put each other on their respective calendars just to see one another.

Now, though, he wanted to throw caution to the wind. He danced his fingers along Joy's spine, feeling the silk of her bare back, and said in a low voice, "Lead the way."

Surprise suffused her face until she broke out in a wide grin. Almost running to his office, she tugged on his hand and then after locking the door, burst into laughter. "You should've seen your face! I've never seen someone so shocked!"

He growled a little and yanked her close. "You shouldn't dare a guy who never backs down from a dare."

"Oh really? I thought you were the guy who rolls his socks in perfect cylinders and irons his underwear for good measure."

"I only iron my silk thongs, and you know it."

"You sure know how to charm a girl," she said on a sigh.

He'd already begun kissing her neck, licking and tasting

the sweetness of her skin. She leaned backward, sighing again. She was wearing some light yellow dress with too many straps and a zipper that didn't seem to exist. When he was about to pull the thing over her head, she yelped and stepped back.

"If you rip my new dress I'll kill you in your sleep." She unbuttoned the front, and he didn't even hear the next words out of her mouth, he was so focused on her breasts encased in light pink lace. "This dress is one-of-a-kind."

"And it's also in the way." He helped her arms out of the straps and tossed the concoction onto a chair. If he had to buy her another one—if he had to buy her twenty new dresses—he'd do it. But looking at her dressed in skimpy lingerie that matched perfectly, Adam's brain essentially shut down.

Joy was, in a word, colorful. From her purple hair to her green eyeliner to her colorful clothing, she could've looked garish and ridiculous. Yet she managed to maintain an elegant, feminine air about her despite the bright plumage. He wasn't sure how she managed it, and he'd never expected to be so obsessed with a woman who was so outlandish compared to his own personality, but he was. From the tattoo on her arm to her nose ring to her purple toenails, he couldn't get enough.

If he thought too much about it, he'd probably turn tail and run.

But right now, he walked her backward until she sat down on his desk. They gazed at each other, breathing heavily, and Adam traced the lines of her tattoo. He had only glanced at it before, but now he studied it, intrigued. Drawn in swaths of purple and blue and lined in black, it was a mermaid with a graceful tail and long, blue hair. It reached from her upper bicep almost to her elbow, an expansive piece that looked alive.

"Why the mermaid?" He traced the strands of the mermaid's hair on her skin.

Joy smiled a little before shrugging. "When I was a kid, I told people I was going to grow up and be a mermaid. Not a doctor or a ballerina." Adam looked up at her, and his heart twisted a little at the expression on her face: uncertainty, perhaps a little sadness.

"But then some brat told me mermaids didn't exist, and that dream ended. So I got the tattoo because I guess I like to think I can do and be anything I want." She shrugged again. "It's cheesy as hell, I know."

He brushed his thumb down the mermaid's tail. Then he leaned forward and kissed her arm. "I like it," he said simply. And he did. He liked *her*. And it was a heady, intoxicating feeling.

She wrapped her arms around his neck. "Thanks. But you're distracting us from the task at hand."

"Which would be?"

"Well, taking off my bra would be a start."

Adam certainly wasn't going to say no to that. Brushing his hands down her back, feeling the curve of her shoulder blades, he found the bra clasp and flicked it open. It sagged in front, and Joy took it off, folding it neatly in his office chair. Her breasts—pale white with pink nipples, already hardened into sweet little berries—were up-thrust, like they were waiting for his touch.

"I always thought of myself as an ass man," he said, "but I'm thinking your breasts are changing my mind."

She laughed. "You're full of shit, but I'll allow it."

She didn't believe him? Then he'd show her, just like he'd said he would. Kneeling on the floor, his head was level with her chest and it gave him perfect access to what he wanted. He cupped both breasts, teasing the nipples, loving how her head tipped back as he played with her. He could just make out light blue veins underneath her skin, pumping blood through her chest.

His touch turned to licking, and he kissed and licked each breast with a thoroughness that had Joy moaning and running her hands through his hair. He shushed her more than once, but when she swatted him on the head, he gave up. No one was close enough to hear them, and at that point, he didn't even care if someone did hear.

He sucked one nipple into his mouth, rolling it around on his tongue. He sucked until Joy trembled and her fingers tightened even harder in his hair. He sucked one then the other until they were red and swollen.

He was so hard he didn't know if he could keep this up much longer, but seeing the glazed look in Joy's eyes? It made the pain of waiting worth it. He wondered if he could make her come just from sucking her nipples. She was so open, so responsive, her body arching and moving, her feet flexing, her eyes closed, that he didn't think he'd ever seen a more beautiful sight.

It suddenly became too much. He stood up and, grabbing her, turned her around. He hooked his fingers into her underwear and tossed them where her dress had landed. Massaging her ass and dipping his fingers into her cleft, they both groaned at how wet she was.

Kissing her neck, he said, "I can't wait any longer."

She shuddered. "Then don't."

He hardly remembered putting on a condom, ripping it open with shaking hands. Joy had leaned down, her elbows on the desk, her ass in the air. She gazed at him under her eyelashes, a flush across her cheeks.

Adam kissed her back, down her spine, even kissing her tailbone, which made her laugh, and then he pushed her down slightly so she was level with his cock. He teased her opening. She was dripping, desperate, and she bucked against him. Her body was a swath of white and pink, soft and silky, her purple hair brushed to one side.

Placing a knee between her legs, he opened her for his onslaught, and he almost came undone from the sight: her glistening sex, waiting for him to fill her. If he weren't hard as a rock already, he'd taste her and make her scream. Instead, he took his cock in hand and slowly fed it into her sheath. She squeaked. He smoothed a hand down her back, slowly, slowly, inching his way inside, and sweat broke out on his forehead.

And then he was fully inside her, his balls touching her sex, and God almighty if he didn't just about lose it right then and there. He gripped her hips, trying to keep her from moving, and he gritted his teeth. He needed to think of ice-cold showers, tax preparation, fertilizer research...

"Adam," Joy said on a long moan. She looked back at him over her naked shoulder, need plain in her expression. She bumped her ass against his pelvis, and that tiny bit of friction sent him over the edge.

He thrust out, slamming back in again. Joy jolted against the desk. He did it again, and again. He had to grip her hips harder to keep her from bucking against him, and he knew he was probably bruising her but he didn't care. She didn't care, either. She moaned into the papers strewn across his desk;

they would be crumpled and useless by the time they were finished.

But he was so close. He thrust harder and harder, the sound of their bodies slapping filling the small office. He hoped she locked the door. Did she lock the door? But then she began thrusting back in time with him, and he lost all thoughts of locked or unlocked doors. He didn't care if everyone in the vineyard opened that door right now. He was too lost in Joy—in her body, her scent, her everything.

"Fuck, Adam, I'm coming." Joy buried her face in her arms, stifling the noises she was making, a combination of a moan and a scream. Adam could feel her body starting to tense. Reaching down between them, he flicked her clit with light strokes as he watched himself fuck her. It was too erotic; it was too much. He couldn't last a second longer.

Then Joy's body bowed and bucked and he could feel the contractions of her sheath clenching his cock. He dug his fingers into her hips. Sweat dripped down his face and was surely soaking his shirt. The room smelled of heat and sex. As the last of her orgasm faded, he thrust one more time and let himself come: he came and came, his balls contracting, filling her until he surely blacked out a little. An exquisite, yet brutal, kind of ecstasy rushed through his blood. His fingers tingled. His head felt light. He heard a buzzing in his ears.

He gently rocked against Joy, lengthening the sensations. He stroked a hand down her spine and then kissed her right on her lower vertebrae. She was still trembling, and she was damp with sweat.

Realizing she was probably uncomfortable, Adam let her go, and she rolled over. A few papers stuck to her breasts and belly; she laughed when she saw them.

Plucking the documents off of her skin, she said, "I hope these weren't important."

He took them and tossed them into the nearby trash. "Not even remotely important," he replied.

"Good." She smiled up at him, and he couldn't help but lean down and kiss her. It was a kiss of tenderness, of gratitude, of hope. He brushed his hands down her arms and she lightly touched his cheek. It was the kind of kiss that was created to devastate your heart.

Adam returned home hours later, still in a daze. He couldn't get the smell of Joy off of him—and he didn't want that scent to ever disappear—but entering his house, full of photos of him and Carolyn, he experienced a feeling of displacement. Like he didn't really live in this place, with its neat furniture and organized kitchen and shelving put together after a memorable outing to Ikea. He didn't even know what he should feel, gazing at a photo of him and Carolyn as his body still shimmered with the memory of Joy underneath him.

He couldn't, he realized, reconcile the two of them right now.

Picking up the photo, he touched Carolyn's face. "What am I doing?" he whispered. The photo, of course, didn't reply, but he felt a little calmer talking to her visage. It wasn't guilt so much as...confusion. He'd been so devastated by his wife's death and the subsequent media circus surrounding it that he'd never expected to find another woman to...what? Sleep with? Date?

He remembered, suddenly, the morning of Carolyn's funeral. It had been a muggy day, and he barely could recall what he'd worn or done before he'd arrived at the church. But as the car parked behind the Methodist church, he'd seen the crowd of strangers. Strangers who turned out to be journalists, jostling the Danvers family for information about Carolyn's untimely death. Had drugs been involved? Was she an alcoholic? Had someone run her off the road and tried to kill her? Adam could remember the sweat glistening on the journalists' foreheads from the unexpectedly warm autumn day, how their hands gripped phones and notebooks and recorders and cameras. How he'd stood mutely, unable to respond. How his dad had growled and pushed them aside and told them if they didn't leave they'd call the cops.

How those same journalists had haunted his and his family's every move for months. Showing up at River's Bend, and Trudy's, at Mike's, even some going so far as to lurk around their property before taking off before the police arrived. He'd been hunted, and all because Carolyn had been a celebrity and people wanted their dirt, no matter who it had hurt.

Adam set the photo down. He remembered Joy's smile as she'd talked to Sadie, telling the girl to have her wedding at the vineyard so Joy could make it into a story. He thought of seeing Carolyn's lifeless body in that casket and the cameras snapping photos of him as he left the funeral.

He brushed moisture from his cheeks, knowing what he had to do.

CHAPTER THIRTEEN

Joy remained on a high that lasted for the rest of the week. She and Adam texted back and forth and saw each other as much as possible, although he was slammed with event planning at River's Bend. Joy found herself writing even more than usual, her muse coming back in full force. If only she'd known that getting good sex would result in her most productive writing spree ever, she would've gone down to the vineyard and seduced Adam ages ago.

She grinned at her laptop. She was practically beaming, and multiple people had commented on it. Grace, for one, who gave her sly glances and teased her as much as possible. Even Mike in the general store had asked what put the spring in her step. Unable to say that she was getting the best boning of her life, she'd replied that it was just Mike's amazing array of produce that sent her into such a euphoric state.

Typing away at her computer, Joy frowned when her phone sounded. And it rang…and rang. She let it go to voice-mail, waiting for the sound that someone had left her a message. No one called her these days, except her mom periodically. But then her phone started ringing again, and she huffed out a breath. She grabbed it from where she'd set it on her kitchen counter, and then she groaned out loud. *Jeremy Evans*, her phone read.

"The fuck is he calling me for?" she growled at the air. She set her phone back down, refusing to answer it. He was not going to ruin her good mood. She wouldn't let him.

Too bad that if anyone knew how to be obnoxiously persistent, it was Jeremy. Her phone rang, and rang, and rang, and she was so irritated that she answered the call with a loud, "What do you want!", not caring if everyone and Mike heard her downstairs.

Jeremy didn't say anything, but then she heard him take a breath. "You picked up!" he said, way too cheerily in her opinion.

She sat back down at her computer, tapping a pen against the desk. "Yeah, after you wouldn't stop calling me. Are you dying? Are you bleeding? If so, call 911. I'm not a nurse, Jeremy."

"No, I'm not dying, but thanks for your concern. I did want to talk to you about something, though."

"Well, considering you refused to leave a voicemail, I assumed you wanted to talk to me." Joy was not in the mood to coddle her cheating ex, and she already regretted picking up the phone. She should've turned her phone on silent and let Jeremy rot, but he also knew how to push her to get what he wanted. She sighed internally.

"I know you aren't happy with me right now," he said slowly, as if measuring out his words. "I get it. But I wanted you to know that I broke up with Regina. We're over."

Joy blinked. Then she tapped her pen faster against her

desk. "Congratulations. Did you cheat on her too?"

"No, but I decided we weren't for each other. We weren't right." Silence. And then, "We were right for each other, though, weren't we?"

Joy set the pen down. She looked out her window onto Main Street, at the few people walking up and down the lane, probably heading to Trudy's for lunch. She thought about Adam and how he'd touched her and kissed her.

"No, Jeremy, we weren't right for each other. No man who cheats on me with my best friend is 'right' for me. Now, are we done here? I have work to do."

"Wait, Jo-Jo! Wait. Just hear me out."

She'd been about to hang up on him, and she cursed that he knew her well enough to know when she'd been about to hang up. She slowly raised the phone back to her ear. Maybe if she let him talk, he'd get out whatever he thought he needed to get out and he'd leave her the hell alone.

"Hear me out for a second. I was in a bad place when...that happened. It's not an excuse, but maybe an explanation. I fucked up. I did. And I'm sorry for it. When I realized that Regina was nothing more than a distraction, I knew I had one more shot."

"One more shot at what?" Joy's voice was filled with dread, because she already knew what he was going to say.

"One more shot at us. I want you back. I want us back together. I love you, Joy. Can you ever forgive me and take me back?"

Peering out the window, she saw the broad shoulders of a man, and she thought it was Adam. But it wasn't. Her heart slowed, and then she raised her fingers to her forehead, realizing she was sweating. She felt clammy and sick to her stomach, and she half-wondered if she was going to puke.

After he'd first cheated on her, Joy had dreamt about Jeremy apologizing and begging for her to come back. She'd loved him—still loved him, in a way—and they had been engaged. He was supposed to have been the man she'd spend the rest of her life with. But all of that had changed when he'd decided to fuck her best friend and then blame her for his straying.

I needed more from you, Joy. And when I didn't get it, I guess I just went somewhere else.

Joy's hand hurt, and she saw that she was clenching the pen so tightly that the plastic had cracked. She set it in the pen stand by her computer.

"Joy, are you there? Joy?"

"I'm here," she said quietly. "I don't know why, but I'm here."

"Oh, good. So, what do you say? Will you at least think about it?"

Her head hurt. Her heart hurt. A tear slipped down her cheek, and she felt guilty about it, swiping at it with quick movements.

"There's nothing to think about. We're over, and I've moved on. Have a good life, Jeremy. But don't contact me again."

She pressed the red button and hung up, instantly turning off her phone to fend off any more calls. Rubbing her eyes, she fought back tears. Why was she crying at all? She didn't want Jeremy back. But he'd reopened wounds that she'd worked so hard to sew up, and now she was bleeding all over the place. Memories she'd shoved away burst through the cracks, and she could only remember the day she'd found out Jeremy had been sleeping with Regina.

She'd been so angry, so angry that it had scared her. She had wanted to scream until her throat was raw, she'd wanted to hurt Jeremy and Regina like they'd hurt her. It had been an explosive anger that she'd never experienced before. *They betrayed me*, she'd kept thinking, over and over again. She'd do the dishes and think, *They betrayed me.* She'd wake up in the morning and think, *They betrayed me.* It was like a poison, filling her veins and slowly killing her. It was only time and distance that had allowed her to recover, but the scars remained.

Joy shut her laptop. She couldn't write anymore today. Jeremy had ruined things—again.

As the afternoon waned on and she drank more wine than was probably wise, she heard a knock on her door and frowned. She wondered if Jeremy had come to haunt her. But when she opened the door, she saw Adam standing there, a look of annoyance on his face.

"What the hell have you been doing all day? I text you and call you for hours, but no response. Is your phone dead?"

She remembered that she'd turned her phone off and never turned it back on. But her mind was mush at the moment, and she just stared at Adam with a blank, tired expression.

He peered at her. "You look like hell. What happened?"

"You're always so charming. Come in." She waved a hand to nowhere in particular, grabbing her oversized glass of wine to continue drinking. She knew she was probably flushed and sweaty from the alcohol, but she was buzzed enough not to care.

"It's only five o'clock and you're drinking. Something's happened. Care to tell me?" He gave her a concerned look.

She shook her head. "I have no interest in talking about anything. Only drinking. You can join, or you can go away." She wandered to her living room, where some Food Network show was playing. One contestant was making a bread pudding, and Joy scoffed. They always made fucking bread pudding because they were hacks. Hacks! She slugged back some more wine.

Adam slowly sat down next to her. He didn't say anything, but Joy had to admit, she felt better with his presence. He was so strong, so put together, despite everything he'd been through. Here she was, crying over her shitty ex, when he'd lost his wife in a tragic accident. He wasn't sitting around drinking and crying.

She wiped away a stray tear and decided she'd feel sorry for herself until the clock struck midnight. Then she'd return to being an adult and throw out her single glass slipper.

Now the tears were coming faster, and she felt so stupid that it made her cry harder.

"Hey, hey, what is this?" Adam put an arm around her shoulders. "What happened? You can't just sit there and cry and expect me to ask nothing about it."

Joy shook her head, crying into his shoulder. She shouldn't indulge herself like this, and yet... It felt good. It felt good to have someone to lean on. She'd been alone for so long lately.

He jostled her. "Hey, come on." He rubbed her arm.

"It's so stupid," she muttered.

"Did Mike run out of Cheetos again? Like that kind of stupid?"

She laughed a watery laugh. "No, but that would make anyone cry. No, it's my ex. He called me and..." She realized she was talking about her ex with her current—boyfriend? lover? her head hurt thinking about it—but at Adam's curious look, she continued. "Jeremy. Did you know I was engaged before I came to Heron's Landing? We were. Jeremy and I. We were together for five years and then he fucks my best friend. So I ended everything and now he has the gall to ask to get back together. What an asshole, right?"

Adam seemed at a loss for words. Then he pulled her closer and brushed a kiss on her forehead. "Definitely an asshole," he murmured.

"I hate him. I hope he chokes on a sandwich and dies."

"Nah, he needs something slower. Like being dismembered."

Joy glanced up and met Adam's gaze. "I had no idea you were so bloodthirsty."

"Only against guys who fuck around like that. And make women cry. He's not worth your tears, Joy." He wiped a tear from her cheek, so gently that it almost made her start crying all over again. "He's a dick. If there's any justice in the world, he'll get chlamydia and have to use Viagra every time he has sex."

Now she laughed. "If only. He already has enough hang-ups about his...Well, never mind." She smiled then, wiping away the last of her tears.

She'd been so afraid to admit to Adam that Jeremy had cheated, but now that it was out in the open, she felt better. Why had she been so freaked out to begin with?

"I didn't want to tell you about Jeremy, you know."

"Why not?"

"Because it's embarrassing. To be cheated on like that. Like, what was so wrong with me that my fiancé would fuck my best friend? You know?"

Adam didn't say anything for a moment, but he stroked the bare skin of her arm. His gaze, though, intensified, his eyes darkening. "You know that's bullshit, right? Cheaters cheat because they're cheaters. Even if you fed him poisoned hamburgers every night, that still doesn't mean he should've cheated."

"I know. But. The whole thing makes me want to shrivel up and die." Joy turned away, Adam's gaze making her uncomfortable. She hated being vulnerable, and admitting that a man she'd loved had screwed her over like that? She couldn't help but blame herself in some way for what had happened.

Adam didn't say anything for a moment. Then he swallowed. "Since we're already talking about our feelings..."

Joy almost laughed, but at his expression, bit her tongue. "Go on," she said softly.

"You know that I don't like journalists. Or, I have a reason for that."

She raised her eyebrows, waiting.

"When Carolyn died..." He looked away, but still kept an arm around her. "When she died, the press hounded us. She was a celebrity, especially around here, and tons of rumors were floating around. Some true, some not. One in particular that popped up was that Carolyn wasn't her father's daughter. That her mother had had an affair."

"But that wasn't true, right?" she asked, confused. "I didn't see anything when I read about Carolyn saying as much."

Adam smiled a little bitterly. "You wouldn't have. We paid off and threatened everyone under the sun not to publish that story. Not to mention, none of them could find any proof or legitimate sources. I know it seems like not a big deal, but for the Young family, it was akin to being caught doing heroin. They've built their empire on wholesome, Midwestern values."

Joy wasn't sure where this was going, but she thought she'd be better off waiting and listening instead of pressing.

"At any rate, the story coming to light forced Carolyn's mother to confess that she *had* had an affair. Carolyn never knew, that we know of, and we'll never know her true parentage. Trenton—her father—threatened divorce, and suffice to say after that, we all pretty much loathed anyone who called themselves journalists. They even went after my parents, practically stalking them for information. For months, I was paranoid about being overheard and even looked in my house for wires and cameras, it was that bad. I hated anyone who reported on the news, even the local weatherman." He finally looked back at Joy and then kissed her forehead. "Until I met you. I was so bitter from that experience it tainted my understanding. I knew there were good writers out there, but I was too angry to see that. You know what I mean?"

She nodded, her throat tight. Her heart ached with his confession, and a part of her was terrified of all of the layers they were shedding as they got closer and closer.

"I understand anger," she said. "I get it, so much. I was so angry with Jeremy after he cheated and wondering what I did wrong..."

"You, Joy McGuire, deserve better than him," Adam said firmly. "The only good thing to come out of this is that he doesn't get to have you. Because you're talented, beautiful, and—"

"And so sexy you can't look at me without getting a boner?"

"No, I was going to say that you're funny, but I guess if you want me to say that you cause me to pitch my tent, sure, that's true, too."

She laughed out loud. Turning, she pulled his head down until his lips reached hers. It was a messy kiss, the angle awkward, but it was one of the best kisses Joy had ever experienced. It was true, and it was fun, and it was filled with a tenderness that she reveled in. He kissed her and licked at her mouth and nipped her bottom lip, and she did the same. The kissed heated up, and soon enough, she was underneath him as he kissed his way down her neck.

"Joy, any man who'd cheat on you is scum of the earth," he said as he kissed her belly button. "You have to know that."

"Mmm, I do now." She shimmied a little, her eyes closed.

When Adam pulled her jeans down to her ankles and kissed her inner thigh, nothing else needed to be said at all. The stubble on his jaw scraped against her sensitive skin, and he stroked and caressed her legs. He kissed the inside of her knee, and he kissed a small scar on her shin. He traced a few stray hairs she'd missed shaving on her ankle. He even kissed her brightly painted toes, neon orange, courtesy of Grace.

Then he slipped his fingers underneath the elastic of her underwear, and she lifted her hips to help him. Adam loved to go down on her, and damn if she didn't love him for it. Jeremy had gone down on her every once in a while, but only when she'd asked. Adam, though, did it without her having to beg, and as he parted her folds and gave her a leisurely lick, she thanked all the gods in existence for sending this man to her.

Any prayers in her mind disappeared as he kissed and licked, sucking at her folds and spreading her moisture across her sex. His thumb dipped inside her; she shivered. Her body tensed, and she grabbed at the pillows on the couch for something to hold onto. But when he mouthed her clit, it didn't matter what she was holding onto: she was lost, completely lost in this man. He played with her. He licked and kissed and thrust a finger inside of her. And then he sucked her clit so hard that her body burst. It burst into pinwheels of light and she bit her hand to keep from screaming out loud.

And thoughts of her ex? Adam had chased them all away.

At Trudy's a few days later, Joy shared a huge plate of pancakes with Adam while stealing sips of his coffee. He kept playing footsie with her under the table, and it was so childish that she couldn't stop laughing.

"Are you serious right now?" she asked, amused and exasperated.

"I'm always serious." His tone was deadpan as he speared another bite of pancake, kicking her lightly.

She pressed down on his foot, but he got free and kicked her a little. She squealed, and as Grace walked by with a raised eyebrow, Joy felt herself blushing.

But the laughter, playing footsie, the pancakes—it all faded away when she heard the door to Trudy's open and a voice she'd know from anywhere ask for a table for one. "I just need a cup of coffee," the voice said, tired, a Chicago accent tingeing his words.

Joy was faced away from the entrance. She stiffened, and she wondered if she were dreaming. But as she heard footsteps, she turned.

And came face to face with the man she'd hoped she'd never see again: Jeremy, her cheating ex-fiancé.

CHAPTER FOURTEEN

As Adam watched the blood drain from Joy's face, he knew instantly who this man was. And at her softly murmured, "Jeremy," his assumption was confirmed. Her ex—this was the guy who'd cheated on her? Adam had to restrain himself from grabbing the guy by the collar and punching him in the face. Instead, he curled his hand into a fist underneath the table.

Jeremy looked like a guy who'd cheat on his fiancée. Tall, lean, his slacks and shirt perfectly ironed and his hair coiffed just so, he looked like he'd cry if you told him he shoes were ugly. Adam hated him on sight.

"Jeremy, what are you...? What are you doing here?" The blood was coming back into Joy's face, but now slashes of red bloomed on her cheeks. Adam could feel her tapping her foot underneath the table.

"I was just in the neighborhood..." Jeremy laughed, fiddling with his collar a little. "I came to see you, Jo-Jo. Why else would I be here in—what is this place called? Heron's Nesting?"

"Heron's Landing," Adam said gruffly.

Jeremy turned toward him, as if just noticing him for the first time. His pale eyebrows raised, he looked from Adam to Joy and back to Adam, as if assessing what, precisely, was their relationship. "And you are?" He didn't hold out his hand, which was probably a good thing, since Adam wanted to break his fingers one by one.

"Jeremy, meet Adam Danvers. He runs and owns the local vineyard here. Adam, this is Jeremy Evans."

"Pleasure," Jeremy drawled, his gaze returning to Joy. "Can we go somewhere private to talk?"

Joy hesitated. She looked at Adam, and he wanted her to say no. *Tell the guy to fuck off,* he thought. But this guy had also been her fiancé, so the history was there. If Adam understood anything, it was the weight of history between two people.

That didn't stop him from being angry that Jeremy was here, in Heron's Landing. And it didn't stop him from seeing red when Joy got up and told Jeremy she'd meet him outside. And it didn't stop him from rising from the booth and slapping some dollars onto the table before stalking outside.

Was she really going to treat this guy like he hadn't broken her heart? He'd seen her tears earlier that week when she'd told him Jeremy had cheated on her. He was scum of the earth, and now he wanted her back?

Fear congealed in his gut. Would she take him back? He couldn't believe she would, but it wouldn't be the first time he'd read someone wrong. He walked toward Mike's, and he could hear Joy's light footsteps behind him.

"Adam! Wait!" She pulled on his arm, steering him to a bench out of earshot. "Let me explain."

Adam gritted his teeth. "There's nothing to explain."

"I know what you're thinking, that I'm being an idiot for even talking to Jeremy. But he's here for a reason, and I know him. If I don't listen to him, he'll keep at it until he gets what he wants. He's one of those people who digs his heels in harder if you tell him no at the outset." Joy shook his shoulder a little, cajoling. "Are you upset?" she finally asked.

He was, and he felt stupid about it. He hated that he was acting like such a hypocrite because he and Joy hadn't made any commitment to each other. But mostly he hated that Joy felt like she had to pacify this asshole ex of hers at all. He took a deep breath. "Haven't you figured out by now that this guy is no good?" he asked quietly.

She didn't react at first, and then she laughed, but it was bitter. "You have a lot of gall to judge me and act miffed that I spoke to another man. Because we're not anything official, are we? You were the one who wanted to keep things quiet, but now when an ex of mine shows up, you're acting jealous and, dare I say it, petty."

Adam whipped his head around, meeting her gaze. Her face was pinched, her cheeks still flushed.

"I'm not being petty," he growled.

"Yes, you are. I have a right to talk to whoever I want. I made no promise to you, and you can't keep me to a made-up promise, either. You can't say you want the milk for free and then bitch and moan when the cow moves onto other pastures!"

"That doesn't even make sense."

"You know what I mean! And you know that Jeremy is the last person I'd invite here. Do you think I wanted him to show up like this? Do you think I'm overjoyed he's here to do God only knows what?"

"I never said you were. But acting like you can talk to him and get somewhere is naïve. He cheated on you with your best friend. Is that all water under the bridge? Will he say he's sorry and you'll take him back?" Adam's voice rose with each word, until he realized he was practically yelling in the street. He saw Joy flinch at his words, and his heart cracked. Why didn't she realize she deserved better?

Her lashes fluttered, and he saw the sheen of tears in her eyes. "Do you really think I'm that stupid?" she asked quietly. "I just told you how I felt about him being here, but it doesn't matter, does it? It's about how *you* feel about everything. How you want to keep things secret." She made a sound in her throat and stood up. "Grow up, Adam. Grow up and realize the entire world doesn't revolve around you and your man-pain."

She stalked off, wiping her eyes as she went. Adam got up to follow, but then he saw Jeremy come up to her and even worse, give her a hug. Adam clenched his fists and turned away.

If he's who she wants, so be it. It's her poor choice.

He walked blindly down Main Street until he reached the end. His car was still parked at Trudy's, but he had no intention of passing by Joy and her shitty ex again. So he walked the handful of miles back to his house, letting the heat and humidity seep into his very pores and maybe exorcise the demons haunting him.

Slamming his front door behind him, he took the bottle of whiskey down from the shelf and poured himself a finger. The alcohol burned on the way down, filling his belly with heat. He wiped his forehead and made growling noises.

He knew, deep inside, he was being exactly what Joy had

153

described him as—selfish and petty. He knew he was being childish. He knew he should apologize and man up. But right that moment, he wanted to drink until the image of Joy and Jeremy embracing faded from his mind completely.

He knew, too, that his reaction indicated that his feelings for Joy ran deeper than he'd known. He couldn't bear the thought of her with another man. It twisted him up inside, like gnarled vines in an overgrown garden, thorny and vicious. His hands shook as he raised his second glass of whiskey to his mouth.

God, I'm an ass, he thought morosely. *A jealous, stupid ass. And an ass who's in love with Joy.*

It wasn't an epiphany that resulted in clouds parting and sun shining through. Instead, it felt more like clouds gathering, stormy and gray, heavy with raindrops. It felt like a collision, an impact that resounded throughout his body and made his limbs throb and ache. It was an oncoming hurricane, and there was nothing he could do to stop it.

It was relentless.

He drank another glass, and another, until it all blurred together, and some of the hurt finally softened around the edges.

The week progressed, and Adam felt as though he ran into Joy and Jeremy everywhere. He shouldn't have been surprised —it was a small town, and he ran into the same ten people regularly—but this felt calculated. Like the universe was laughing at him: *look at the woman you love with the man who betrayed her! Isn't it hilarious?*

Hilarious, he thought. He gritted his teeth until his jaw hurt when he saw the two of them talking, their faces close. He clenched his fists until his arms hurt when he saw Joy laugh at something Jeremy said. And he banned himself from going to Trudy's for the rest of the week because seeing them eating together was like being knocked flat on his ass.

It didn't take long for everyone in Heron's Landing to know that Joy McGuire's ex-fiancé had arrived and was making headway to getting her back. It also didn't take long for everyone to murmur about what had happened between him and Joy—it was the town's worst kept secret—and some even wondered if Adam and Jeremy would have a battle to fight things out. What kind of battle, they weren't sure, but maybe some kind of wrestling match. Or even an old-fashioned duel, pistols and all.

At any rate, Joy and Jeremy were the hot topic of the town. Whispers followed wherever they went. The only consolation Adam felt was that Jeremy was staying at the one inn in Heron's Landing instead of at Joy's place. He liked to think they weren't already sleeping together, but it didn't help him feel much better.

Late one evening, Adam entered Mike's for a few things, and he almost turned around and left sans milk when he spotted Joy and Jeremy in one of the aisles. Joy's purple hair stood out in the beige confines of the store, and Adam's heart twisted. He'd missed her. Watching them, he saw Jeremy point at something and then Joy rolled her eyes. She didn't seem particularly happy to be with him, her face pinched and her forehead creased, which bolstered Adam's mood enough to allow him to enter the store to get what he needed.

"Joy," he said as he passed them. The store was so small that there was no way they could avoid each other. "Jeremy," he added as an afterthought.

"Hi, Adam," Joy replied. She glanced at Jeremy, but he only nodded tightly and looked away.

"Do you want me to leave?" Adam overheard Jeremy asking, and his ears pricked up. Looking at the milk selection, he suddenly needed to look at each brand and kind carefully. Did he want one percent or two percent or maybe even whole milk?

"I never said that," Joy replied.

"You implied it."

"Look, I didn't invite you here. You know that. And I already told you no." Her voice was a low whisper, almost a hiss in the confines of Mike's.

Adam stared harder at the jugs of milk.

"I know you didn't, but I'm here. Can't we work something out?" Jeremy's voice was pleading, and Adam sneered at the sound. Was he really begging Joy to take his cheating ass back? He hoped she kicked him to the curb and left him to cry.

"No, we can't. And I don't want to talk about this here."

Adam stiffened, feeling Joy's gaze on his back. He plucked a carton of milk from the fridge and then snagged a bag of chips on his way to the register, where Mrs. Ferry was buying her own snacks for the evening.

"Fine. I'm going back to the hotel."

Adam turned his head slightly to watch Jeremy stalk out of the store, and he couldn't stop from snorting out loud. Would the man throw a temper tantrum, too?

As he was paying, he watched Joy out of the corner of his eye. Her shoulders were slumped, and she looked exhausted. He wanted to take her into his arms and make all of her worries disappear. Could he really be petty enough to ignore her when she clearly didn't want her shitty ex here in the first place?

He was about to approach her when Jeremy appeared again. "You're still here?" he said with a sneer when he saw Adam. "Come on," he said to Joy, "let's get out of here."

"Do you not want anything?"

"No. We'll get it later. When we're not being watched."

Jeremy tried to take hold of Joy's wrist, but she wouldn't let him. She looked at Adam for a brief moment. Her eyes were sad, and tired, and maybe a little hopeless.

Adam hated that.

THE FOLLOWING Friday dawned bright and muggy. It was now officially August, and the grapes had begun to ripen until they'd be ready in October. They would know for certain what the harvest would look like come the fall. Adam awoke that morning, grim-faced and hoping that he'd been wrong about how bad the crop was. Maybe once they harvested it, it would look better than expected.

But getting to River's Bend that morning, he saw the look on Chris's face, and he knew things weren't good. He followed his manager out into the fields, and they looked at the vines. The number of green grapes beginning to turn into purple ones was disheartening. It was still early days, though, and all they could do was wait and see what the crop yielded in October.

Today, though, Adam could only see River's Bend falling apart into the river below, and all of his grandfather and father's hard work being done for naught. He knew the weather hadn't been his fault, but it wasn't much of a consolation.

"We'll figure it out," Chris said quietly, a hand to his forehead as he looked out onto the vineyard.

"Yeah, we will," Adam replied, unconvinced.

He still had the upcoming wedding to plan. It was scheduled for the middle of November, after the harvest. Returning to his office, Adam passed Jaime, who slapped him on the shoulder and nodded. He appreciated that his friend never tried to give him false hope, but instead just indicated he was there for him. He hoped Jaime knew that he could count on Adam as well.

Adam made calls and talked with Sadie about her wedding, confirming a few random details. He then made financial projections for next year, which were so depressing that he almost banged his forehead against his desk in frustration.

He wished Joy were here. She'd make this situation better. Even if she just smiled and kissed him, everything would seem hopeful.

Adam rolled his eyes at himself. He was being both pathetic and lovesick. He needed to focus on his damn business, but thoughts of Joy popped into his mind periodically throughout the day no matter what he did. It was a sickness, really, and one he honestly didn't want a cure for.

At the end of the day, he shut off his computer and wondered if his parents would be too mad if he skipped out on family dinner that night. But all thoughts of dinner and his parents fled when Jaime came into his office, shut the door, and looked so grim he wondered if someone had died.

"What happened?"

Jaime clenched his jaw. He didn't say anything, like he was

trying to figure out how to say it, and it only made everything worse.

Adam went around the desk and saw that Jaime had his phone clutched in his right hand. "What the fuck is it? Is someone hurt? Dead?" He thought of when the cop had come and told him Carolyn had hit that tree, and the blood drained from his face.

"Oh Christ, no. No one is hurt or dead. I'm sorry." Jaime let out a breath. "But I saw this and, well, I thought you needed to see it for yourself." He handed him his phone, which was open to some website.

"Are you showing me your dating profile?" Adam tried to joke. "I guess I could see why you'd looked like you were going to throw up…" When he saw the words at the top of the page, though, and then kept scrolling, all jokes fled. His head buzzed. And he kept reading the words, over and over again, because they just wouldn't compute.

CAROLYN DANVERS: WIFE, PHILANTHROPIST…AND NOT HER FATHER'S DAUGHTER?

Adam's blood ran cold. He glanced through the article, the article they'd fought so hard to keep from coming to light.

And now it was exposed to the entire world. Adam had never cared who Carolyn's father was, but he knew how important it had been to the Young family to keep that quiet, especially in the wake of her death.

"Adam? Say something. You're freaking me out."

He knew, suddenly, with such a painful clarity that he felt weak in the knees, who had done this. He *knew*. He'd told her this information in confidence and she'd betrayed him. There was no name attached to the story, but that didn't matter.

He shoved the phone back into Jaime's hands. "I have to go."

"Wait, what are you going to do? Do you know who did this?"

"I know exactly who did it." When Jaime looked blank, he just stared at him.

Jaime's brows rose and he whistled. "Do you mean Joy? How can you know that for sure? She doesn't strike me as the type. I know you're pissed, and you should be, but don't burn bridges before you really know."

"I told her about Carolyn's secret. She's the only person who knew outside of the family, and the only person with something to gain from knowing." He slammed his hand down onto his desk. "I was so fucking stupid. I trusted her, even though I already knew journalists like her..." He grabbed his phone from his desk. "I have to go."

Jaime said to his retreating back, "Good luck. And I hope you're wrong. For your sake, and Joy's."

CHAPTER FIFTEEN

Joy realized quickly that Jeremy had no intention of leaving soon and that if it weren't illegal, she would've strangled him by the end of the first day of his coming to Heron's Landing.

She'd cajoled, she'd asked, she'd ordered, she'd done everything she could to get him to leave. But if Jeremy were talented at anything at all, it was being stubborn. And he'd gotten it into his brain that if he just stuck things out, Joy would finally surrender and they could be together again.

Not a very romantic thought, but there it was. He wanted her so exhausted that she'd capitulate and then they could somehow be happy again.

The first day, when Jeremy had shown up at Trudy's and Adam had stalked off, Joy had almost abandoned Jeremy in the middle of Main Street to go after Adam. But she knew Jeremy: he'd find her, and if he couldn't find her, he'd make life hell for everyone else in Heron's Landing.

As she sat with him at Trudy's and he ordered a

hamburger in a snide voice, she wondered how she ever put up with him, let alone thought she'd marry him.

She watched him as he ate, swirling his fries in mustard—one of his weird quirks—and she told herself he hadn't been so bad years earlier. And it was true, at least partially. Jeremy had grown harder and more cynical with the passing years, and he'd taken it out on everyone else around him. His job, the lack of real writing opportunities, the lack of promotion, the lack of money—everything had added up and he'd decided it was the world that was against him, as opposed to him not working hard enough or simply accepting that not everything went the way you wanted it to.

His immaturity, Joy knew, had created this man-child that Jeremy was now. Just recently turned thirty, he looked younger, with his polo shirts and gelled hair, like they were still in college. She watched him eat and how he didn't close his mouth as he chewed. She'd always hated that. But now it was…unbearable.

Jeremy wiped his fingers on his pants and looked around for their waitress. "Do you ever get any service in this place?"

"When you're nice to the servers, sure," Joy replied.

"Huh." He turned his gaze back to her. "So I'm sure you're wanting to know why I'm here."

"Something like that."

He leaned forward, his face intent. Joy instinctively stilled herself for the oncoming impact.

"I told you that I broke up with Regina, right? When I left her place, I knew I had to get you back."

"Because you needed someone to do your laundry now that Regina was out of the job?"

He waved away her sarcasm. "I know you're still mad. But

you should look at my side of things: I gave up something good to come back to you. I didn't have to. But I'm here. Shouldn't that count for something?"

It was a rare thing for Joy to be at a complete loss for words, but at the moment, she didn't know what to say. The only word swirling in her mind was *fuck fuck fuck fuck*, and maybe tossing her water glass in Jeremy's face. But anytime she got emotional, Jeremy tended to dismiss what she was saying.

She knew now that that had been one of his many shitty tactics. God, how had she dated him for so long without realizing how terrible he was as a person?

"I already told you," she said calmly, "I'm not interested in getting back together. I don't want to return to Chicago, either. So you've wasted money on this trip if that was your only reason for coming here."

"What, did you think I came here for, the scenery? The sad little vineyard?" Jeremy stuffed some dollars into the leather folder with the bill and stood up. "Come on, let's take a walk."

As he left Trudy's, Joy made sure to add a few more dollars for a tip—as he didn't believe in tipping—and followed after him. Grace eyed her as she left, and Joy could only shrug and go after him. She had to at least make sure to minimize the damage he could do in Heron's Landing as much as possible, and if it meant having to babysit him for a while? So be it.

Knowing that his current tactics weren't working, Jeremy apparently decided to try being charming. He took Joy's hand and said conversationally, "How have you liked it here? I guess I could see the appeal. You can even park without circling the block for an hour!"

She smiled a little. "It was a big change, and I do miss the food in Chicago. But it's been a welcome change."

"How about the vineyard? Have you been there?"

At the mention of River's Bend, her heart contracted. Did Adam think she was going to take Jeremy back? After everything she'd told him about her ex? She wished he were here. He'd tell her everything was going to be all right and then pull her close. It was cheesy and stupid, but she'd never felt as safe as she did in his arms.

"I have, a few times. It's gorgeous, and their wine is amazing. You'd never think somewhere in nowhere Missouri they'd have wine like that, but you'd be surprised."

Jeremy was looking around, wrinkling his nose at a beat-up pickup outside the hardware store. "Sounds positively adorable. Who was that guy you were with when I came into the restaurant?" His tone sounded vaguely interested, but she could hear jealousy lacing his voice regardless.

"That was Adam Danvers. He owns and runs River's Bend —the vineyard."

"Oh really? Is he married?"

Joy raised her eyebrows at the question. Since when did Jeremy care about someone's marital status? Now that she thought about it, Adam hadn't been wearing his wedding ring lately. "He was," she replied slowly, "but his wife died in a car accident."

"Adam Danvers, Adam Danvers." Jeremy repeated the name, like he was tasting it on his tongue. Then he made an a-ha! sound. "I know that name! Was he married to one of the Youngs, of Young and Co.? I remember a story about their wedding."

"He was—Carolyn was her name." Joy narrowed her eyes. "You have a good memory."

He shrugged. "Comes with the territory. You know what I mean." He grinned.

Jeremy was also a writer, although his writing tended more toward gossip columns and celebrity exposes. Although Carolyn Danvers nee Young hadn't been an A-list celebrity by any means, she'd still been fairly famous, especially in Midwestern circles. And if anyone would've known the name, it would be Jeremy.

The rest of the week dragged on, as Jeremy continued to extend his stay. Everyday, he made a case for him and Joy to get back together. And everyday, she turned him down. By the third day, she gave him an ultimatum: he could either stop asking her, or he could leave. It was his choice.

For some strange reason, he decided to stay. He continued to ask her things about Heron's Landing, about River's Bend, about the Danvers family, about Adam. They visited the vineyard briefly, although thankfully they didn't run into Adam.

By the fifth day, Jeremy had apparently gotten enough of small-town life and told Joy that morning that he was taking a flight out of St. Louis later that afternoon and would be leaving after breakfast. She'd never been so happy to see another person leave.

His suitcase packed and wearing one of his many polo shirts, Jeremy embraced her before leaving. She lightly patted his shoulder. "See you, Jo-Jo," he said into her neck. "I'll call you when I land."

She sighed. "Bye, Jeremy."

After he drove away in his rental car, Joy decided to call

her phone company and change her number. She never, ever, wanted a repeat of the last few days.

Joy was also well aware of the town whispering about her being with Jeremy these past few days. She'd heard rumblings that she was dumping Adam for her ex-fiancé, and she wanted to scream aloud that they knew nothing. But if she'd learned anything about small-town life, it was that trying to combat a rumor head-on by denying it had a tendency to make the rumor grow even faster.

The next few days passed in a blur. Joy tried to get back into the swing of things. She texted Adam to tell him about her new number, but he only replied in a clipped *okay.* She tried writing a post for the Heron's Landing blog, but she deleted it after a few paragraphs.

At home one evening sipping wine and watching *The Bachelor,* she got a text from Grace: *did you see this?* The text included a link. Frowning, Joy tapped the link. And then her eyes widened, and then she gasped. Horror filled her as she read the headline.

CAROLYN DANVERS: WIFE, PHILANTHROPIST...AND NOT HER FATHER'S DAUGHTER?

She scrolled through the article, reading it so quickly she hardly comprehended its content, but the headline was enough. She looked at the author—an E. Jones, how helpful— and then she read the article more slowly. The blood drained from her face as she read the words, and she knew who the real author was.

Jeremy. Jeremy had done this.

Had he come to Heron's Landing for this sole purpose? No, he hadn't known, but when she'd mentioned Adam, he'd realized that he could maybe find some dirt. And look at the dirt he'd been able to uncover! The secret Adam had told her and she'd promised never to tell. And she hadn't—but it didn't look like that.

She called Grace, her entire body trembling. "Has he seen it?" she asked without saying hello.

She heard Grace sigh. "I don't know, but I would bet he has already."

Joy groaned. "This is terrible. You know I didn't do this, right?"

"I know. I'm not sure a lot of other people will give you the benefit of the doubt, though." Grace's voice was sad and heavy. "Everyone loved Carolyn around here, and now that you were seen with Jeremy all week…"

Joy's chest tightened; she felt like she couldn't breathe. The town's opinion of her had already taken a hit, and now this? They'd assume the worst. And it made sense, didn't it? Joy was a journalist, just like the ones who'd made the Danvers' family life hell for months after Carolyn's death.

She was going to be sick. "I have to go," she said to Grace and hung up.

Should she go to Adam's? Try to explain? She had no idea how Jeremy had gotten this information, but she'd find out. She'd wring his neck and throw him into Lake Michigan. At that thought, she felt a little bit better—but not much.

Her question was answered when a knock sounded on her door. She knew those footsteps, and she could feel Adam's anger through the wood. When she opened the door, he stood in front of her, his face flushed, his nostrils flared. He looked livid.

"Joy," he said.

"Adam. Come in." She shut the door behind him. Before he

could say anything, she said, "I'm so sorry. So sorry. I feel sick. Grace sent me the link."

His back was to her, and she could see how stiff it was. He seemed like he were made of marble: impenetrable, cold. He didn't say anything, though.

"You have to know, you have to believe me," she said as she touched his arm, "that I had nothing whatsoever to do with this. I know it was Jeremy, and I'm so sorry he would betray you and Carolyn and everyone in this town for himself. If I'd had any idea he was going to do this I would've stopped it." She gripped his arm, trying to make him see and understand. "Adam, please say something."

When he remained silent, she let him go. She stuffed her hands into her pockets. She wasn't going to beg. Why did he come here, if he was just going to stand there and judge?

"I can't look at you," he said.

Joy flinched.

"I didn't want to believe it. I wanted to think there was some misunderstanding. But I'm not that naïve. I can't be." He finally turned to her, and the pain in his eyes shot an arrow through her. "You were the only one who knew about Carolyn, and the only one who had something to gain from it. No reporter could ever get definitive proof because the family was the only source. And then you. So, tell me, how could that article be published without your help?"

Joy made a sound, between a growl and a sob. "I don't know! You have to believe me: I told Jeremy *nothing*. Why would I? How could I betray you?" Tears filled her eyes, and she couldn't stop them from spilling over. "I love you," she whispered. "I love you, Adam. How could you think I'd betray you like that?"

"People who love you betray you all the time."

"And so that's it? I've been judged and found wanting without any real evidence?" She wiped her eyes, knowing her mascara would be smeared all over her cheeks, but she didn't care. "I'm just a slut for hire, right? Just a writer out to screw everyone else over for a few bucks? Isn't that what you said when we first met?"

Adam closed his eyes. "I never called you a slut."

She smiled, bitter and sad. "You implied it. That I have no ethics or morals." She stepped toward him, and looking up into his wretched, wonderful face, she asked, "You were waiting for this, weren't you? For the moment you could justify thinking that journalists are only out to get you. You were waiting for the ax to fall this entire time, am I right?" She studied his face, her gaze roving over the beautiful lines of his jaw and nose and the stubble on his cheeks and how his hair was overgrown and needed a trim and how he had a tiny mole on his right ear. "Can you deny it?"

"I didn't—I never wanted this. I wanted to think you were different. But I refuse to play the fool when it's all right there in front of me."

He sounded choked, and Joy knew she saw tears in his eyes. She wanted to simultaneously hug him and slap him, she was so frustrated. And hurt. And betrayed.

"So my word means nothing then."

When he didn't reply, she had her answer.

"You think you have it all figured out. I'm the bad guy. I'm the one who came here to seduce you and use you. Even though I told you that I love you, you throw it back into my face. Did you care about me at all? Or did you go home, disgusted, after you'd slept with me?"

That got him to move. He grabbed her by the arms: his fingers dug into her biceps, not enough to hurt, but enough to get her attention. "You never disgusted me. I wanted you the moment I first saw you. I still want you. I dream about you and Jesus Christ, Joy, don't you know the goddamn truth? I love you so much it kills me, and it kills me that you did this and that I love you still."

"Fuck you, Adam Danvers," she whispered. "Fuck you and everything you think you stand for."

He growled, and he covered her mouth with his. She wanted to resist, she wanted to slap him so hard he saw stars, but she only surrendered and kissed him back. She knew it would be the last time. So she kissed him with everything she had inside: with lips and tongue and teeth and groans and emotions spilling out from every crevice. It was the single most devastating kiss she'd ever had in her life.

They pulled away, breathing hard. Adam's hands were still on her arms, but when he realized this, he let go. He stepped away. He wiped his mouth.

"I shouldn't have done that," he said. "I'm sorry."

The tears wouldn't stop. They flowed down her cheeks and dripped down her chin. "You're sorry? Oh, Adam. You're so convinced that the world is out to get you that you'll destroy yourself to prove that point." She sobbed. "You break my heart."

They stood silent, Joy crying, Adam wiping his eyes. She wanted him to leave. She wanted him to stay. She knew, with the knowledge that tore her apart, that it was over.

Over before it had really even begun.

"I need you to go," she said finally. "Please, go. I know you think I wrote this article, but I didn't. I hope someday you can believe that."

He gazed at her, and he clenched his fists at his side. He looked like he wanted to touch her. Then he sighed.

"Bye, Joy."

The image of his back, of his slumped shoulders, the sound of the door closing, would haunt Joy for weeks to come. After locking the door behind him, she collapsed against it, sobbing so hard it hurt her chest and throat. She cried so hard she made gasping, choking sounds, and she knew Mike could probably hear her downstairs. She didn't care. She cried until she couldn't cry anymore.

She then slumped down on the floor, arms around herself, and stared at the sudden emptiness of her apartment. And she knew that her time in Heron's Landing was over.

CHAPTER SIXTEEN

"So, what, are you just going to hide for the next six months?"

Joy sighed. "Do you have a better idea?"

"I'm thinking you should get coffee with me and act like you did nothing wrong—which you did. Do nothing wrong, that is."

Grace's matter-of-fact voice bolstered Joy's depressed spirits a little, but that didn't stop the proverbial storm clouds from gathering over her still. In a town as small as Heron's Landing, news traveled fast, and everyone and their dog had read the exposé about Carolyn. Since Adam had accused Joy of writing it, now everyone else in the town believed she'd written it, as well. The only person who thought she was innocent was Grace.

A week later, and things had only gotten worse. Joy barely left her apartment, afraid of the looks and whispers that accompanied her everywhere she went. She couldn't even go into Mike's downstairs without someone looking at her like she killed their firstborn.

"I don't really want coffee," she said to Grace. "I just want to sleep."

"You need to get out of your apartment. Also, your hiding makes it look like you're guilty. I know it's not fair, but that's just how it is."

Joy looked down at her current outfit—pajama shorts, a ratty t-shirt, her hair unwashed—and she sighed again. "I guess I'll put on a bra and see you in a bit."

"Good. Maybe brush your teeth, too."

"Haha. See you in a bit."

Sniffing her breath, Joy realized that maybe she should swish with some Listerine just in case. She pulled on her comfiest bra, splashed her face with cold water, and slipped her feet into her beat-up flip-flops to walk the block down to Trudy's.

It was a beautiful, albeit hot, August day. Humid and bright, Joy wished she'd remembered her sunglasses. She squinted, and it was so bright that she didn't see the few townsfolk that were walking about staring at her. But as she got closer to Trudy's, she saw the salon owner Dana frown in her direction. Joy gave a wave; Dana ignored it and walked in the opposite direction.

So that was going to be how it was from now on, was it? Joy McGuire, the woman who betrayed Saint Adam, and who wrote dirt about his angelic dead wife. It didn't matter if she denied writing it: Adam believed it, and thus Heron's Landing believed it.

The door chimed when she entered Trudy's, and she ignored the stares from the four people already seated. One couple was Sadie and Robert, and Joy could hear Sadie whisper something under her breath, Robert grunting in some kind of agreement.

Joy slid into the booth opposite Grace. The girl had already ordered coffee for the both of them, and at the smell, Joy had to restrain herself from crying. Maybe she'd needed coffee more than she'd known.

"You look terrible," Grace said. "Have you eaten at all this week? Taken a shower?"

"Nice to see you, too. I took a shower yesterday. I think I ate two days ago. Thanks for asking, though."

Grace's forehead creased in concern. "Have you talked to Adam?" she asked quietly.

Joy shook her head. She couldn't think about him right now. Whenever she did, she wanted to scream, and then she wanted to cry, and then she wanted to go to his house and kick him the balls. But mostly it just *hurt*.

It hurt to have the man you loved believe that you were a liar.

"At first I kept calling him, because I just wanted him to believe me. I couldn't let him think that I'd do something like that, you know? But when he kept ignoring me, I stopped." Joy smiled, a sad, bitter smile. "I'm not going to beg. I know I'm innocent. That'll have to be enough." She sipped the coffee, and the warmth of it helped ease a little bit of the tension in her body.

"He's being such a stupid asshole. I tried talking to him, but he kicked me out. I knew he was touchy about journalists, but this…" Grace stirred her coffee so vigorously some of it spilled onto the table. "This takes it to another level. If you want to push him off a cliff, I'll gladly help you."

"Thanks, hun."

They sat and drank their coffee in silence, mostly undisturbed. One of the few benefits of living in the Midwest, Joy thought, was that everyone was trained to be so nice that they'd never say anything rude to your face. So although most everyone in Trudy's at that moment were thinking bad things about her, no one had the balls to tell her off.

Joy sipped her coffee. Sometimes ignorance really was bliss.

That bliss, however, was shattered when Sadie and Robert walked passed them to the exit. To Joy's surprise, Sadie stopped, Robert bumping into her with a grunt.

"You know," Sadie said, her voice shaking with anger, "I can't believe you'd do something so horrible. Hasn't Adam—" Sadie gestured at Grace now "—and the entire family gone through enough? You should be ashamed of yourself."

Joy blinked. So much for thinking no one here would say something to her face. She gripped her coffee cup, her mind scrambling for a reply, but Grace beat her to it.

"You don't know anything, Sadie. I'd recommend you keep your nose out of other people's business, and maybe focus on your own issues. Weren't you the one talking about 'throwing the first stone' at church earlier this month? Maybe you should take your own advice." Grace had stood up in the booth, but now she sat back down, fists clenched.

Sadie made incredulous noises in the back of her throat. Then, to everyone's astonishment, Robert said, "She's right, Sadie. Joy, Grace, sorry about that." In a lower voice, he added, "Let's go."

Robert hustled his fiancée out the door, the chime ringing at their exit. The few people in the diner still said nothing, silence filling the restaurant.

Joy, though, could only feel one thing: exhaustion. And with that exhaustion came the realization that she couldn't stay here.

Heron's Landing was no longer her safe place to land.

It broke her heart, thinking that. After crying her eyes out when Adam had left her apartment, she thought she'd try to ride things out. But now she saw that had been naïve. She hated that leaving would seem like running away. How could she stay in a place that hated her guts? She wasn't enough of a masochist to stay and be harassed like this.

And Adam... She squeezed her eyes shut. That was over. Staying wouldn't change that.

"What the hell was that?" Jaime stepped up to their booth, looking like he'd just gotten out of the shower. Joy had seen him jogging past her apartment multiple times for his morning run; she assumed he'd just finished his run for today. "What did Sadie say to you guys?"

Grace looked up at him and turned a bright red. Joy almost laughed, but it hurt too much to laugh right now. "She thought she should tell me I'm a terrible person," Joy replied. "Just another regular day around here."

Jaime swore. "Is this happening a lot? I have to talk to him about this."

"No, don't. Please. It's not worth it." Joy looked up into Jaime's face, and the concern in his expression made her chest constrict. "Besides, I'm leaving, anyway."

Grace gasped. Her coffee cup tipped over, but luckily, it was already empty. "You can't leave! Where will you go? Please don't leave!"

"How can I stay here? You saw what just happened. I'm not welcome here." Joy covered Grace's hand with hers and squeezed. "That doesn't mean we can't stay in touch, though."

Grace looked like she was about to start crying. She squeezed Joy's hand back and then slumped back into her booth.

"Are you sure that's the wisest decision?" Jaime asked. Suddenly realizing standing over them was rather awkward, he sat down next to Grace, who scurried as far away from him as she could. He didn't notice. "I think this will blow over soon enough."

"Do you really think so? I don't. Small towns have long memories. I do appreciate your support, though. You don't really know me, but, thank you." Joy finished her coffee; it had already gone cold. "I'll go back to Chicago for now. And figure out things after that."

"Are you sure? Chicago?" Grace stared at her, and then she bit her lip.

Joy knew she was talking about Jeremy. But Joy refused to avoid an entire city just because her shitty ex happened to be lurking in it. Besides, she had unfinished business to attend to there.

"I have to go. But I'll let you know what I end up deciding. Eat some pancakes for me, okay?"

"I'll make sure she eats something," Jaime replied. "What'll you have, Grace?"

Grace only covered her face in her hands and sighed.

TWO WEEKS LATER, Joy stood outside in the late August heat and watched her things being moved again. Had it really only been two months she'd been here? It had felt like an eternity, and yet also like the blink of an eye.

Looking up and down Main Street, she had to admit, she'd miss this place. She could've seen herself staying here for good. But now she was running back to the place she'd run from. How was that for ironic?

"Joy!"

She stiffened. She'd know that voice anymore—it was the voice that haunted her dreams most nights. She turned, and she had to stifle the sob from crawling up her throat.

Adam walked up to her. He looked…tired. Thin. Pale. A part of her was upset by this, but another part felt vindicated. She was glad he'd been as miserable as she'd been.

"Are you really leaving?"

She stared at him. He'd refused to talk to her for weeks, and now he showed up acting brand new? She couldn't help it: she laughed.

He reared back. "What…?"

"Now you're going to act like you care? Go home, Adam. My movers are almost done and I have to get on the road." She turned away, staring resolutely at the guys hauling her couch into the truck.

By the silence, she almost thought he'd left. But then he said, "Are we just going to end things like this?"

"*You* ended things, remember? You were convinced I wrote that story. So please, save me the sob story." When she felt his hand on her arm, she wrenched herself away. Anger sparked in her gut. She whirled on him. "Leave. Me. Alone," she hissed.

His mouth tightened. "Fine. Although I'm the one who should be mad, you know."

"Of course! You're always the victim! Go home and be sad. I'm busy."

She knew it was mean, and petty, but she was done. She just wanted to get out of here. Get as far away from Adam Danvers as she could. Tears threatened, but she blinked them away. She wasn't going to cry over him anymore.

"I meant what I said, you know," he murmured. "I loved you. I still do. I hope you can be happy, Joy."

Did he want to break her heart even more than he already had? She bit her lip so hard she tasted blood. "You too, Adam," she forced herself to say.

When she finally got onto the highway, the moving truck following her, she cried until she reached the Illinois border. But as she entered her home state again, she vowed to herself: she wouldn't shed another tear over Adam Danvers.

And when she arrived in Chicago, she kept that vow.

AUGUST PASSED INTO SEPTEMBER, and Joy felt as though she were moving through a fog. Even in the hustle and bustle of Chicago, she couldn't seem to find her center. She saw Adam everywhere: in the bright green trees near Lake Michigan; in the laugh of a man down the street; in the bottles of wine she looked at in the grocery store. She couldn't escape him, no matter how much she wanted to.

Two weeks after Labor Day was when she got up the courage to call the person she needed to talk to most: her former best friend, Regina.

She and Regina had met when Joy had moved to Chicago as a young college graduate, and they'd been inseparable. Joy,

Regina and then Jeremy had become a trio, going everywhere together. Joy had never thought her friend held the slightest interest in her boyfriend-turned-fiancé, but maybe she just hadn't been paying attention.

Now that she was back in town, though, Joy needed to see her friend. It didn't make sense, she knew, but Joy was lonely. She'd missed her friend, and now that Jeremy was out of the picture, maybe they could, at the very least, talk.

They decided to meet at a coffee shop they'd gone to many times before. When Joy arrived, Regina hadn't gotten there yet, so she took a table in the back and ordered a latte with an extra shot. Her heart pounding, she didn't know what to expect when Regina arrived. But when she did walk into the shop, Joy had to stifle a gasp.

Regina had lost weight—so much that she seemed sickly. She'd also cut her hair short, and her clothes hung loosely about her frame. When she saw Joy, she smiled a little but then as if realizing everything that had happened, the smile faded. She awkwardly pulled out the chair at the table and sat down, clutching her purse.

Regina had always been a striking woman, with high-lighted brown hair and blue eyes. Joy had never seen her without mascara or her hair brushed, but now she looked as if she'd just rolled out of bed. Despite herself, Joy's heart contracted. What had happened since Jeremy had dumped her?

"Do you want anything?" Joy asked.

Regina looked up, startled. She looked like she was about to fiddle with her hair, but then realizing she'd cut it all off, she shrugged. "I'm okay."

"Okay." Joy got up to get her latte, her mind whirling.

The pair's conversation was stilted at best, with both accidentally interrupting the other. Regina briefly mentioned that she was doing ad work for a local marketing agency, but otherwise, she offered little detail. Joy similarly hedged around what had happened in Heron's Landing.

Now they were at a stalemate. Joy suddenly wished she hadn't called Regina at all. What did it matter? They could never be like they used to.

"I went to that sushi place we used to go to all the time," Regina blurted. She blushed a little, but added, "You know, the one with the hot waiter?"

Yes, Joy remembered. The place was known for its good-looking staff, and this waiter was so gorgeous that Regina and Joy had eaten sushi every other day for three whole months before Jeremy had come into the picture.

"Remember when you gave him your number, and he thought you were propositioning him?" Regina laughed, although it sounded rusty. "I'll never forget the look on your face."

"I was so embarrassed that I tried to leave without paying," Joy said, a wry smile curving her lips. "And they called the cops on us. I said that we could never go back there again."

"Well, I went there last week, but no hot waiter. I guess he moved onto greener pastures."

Joy smiled at Regina, who smiled back. Memories flooded Joy, and she wished all of sudden to forget the past, to move on. She'd missed her friend. And she obviously hadn't had a good time of it, either.

"What happened, Regina?" Joy asked quietly. "What happened? To us? To all of us?"

Regina messed with the handles of her purse, curling them

about her fingers like a cat's cradle. "I don't know. It just...I don't know. But I'm so sorry for everything. I don't deserve your forgiveness, but I do want you to know how sorry I am."

Joy swallowed sudden tears. Seeing Regina's agitation, Joy reached out and touched her hand. "I know you are. I don't know when I'll get there, but I do know I'd like my friend back someday."

After that, the two of them opened up more than they had earlier. Joy admitted to Jeremy coming to Heron's Landing, which Regina had known nothing about. Then when she told her about Jeremy betraying her and writing the story about Adam's wife, Regina looked like she could get up and find Jeremy herself and beat him to a pulp.

"That disgusting little shit!" she hissed. "He has balls made of steel, I will say that."

"Well, he definitely thought he'd get away with it."

Regina fidgeted, biting her lip. She looked like she was trying to figure out if she should admit something or not. Then she let out a breath. "I'll probably get my ass reamed for this, but you should know: there's been an investigation into some of Jeremy's stories. There are rumors of plagiarism and scalping other journalists' stories." Regina swallowed. "I could lose out on clients for admitting this, though, so, keep it on the down low?"

Joy couldn't believe what she was hearing. Jeremy, stealing other writers' work? Then again, he obviously didn't care about ethics. For the first time in weeks, she saw a light at the end of the tunnel. If she could hurt his credibility, maybe, just maybe, she could repair her own.

And maybe she could convince Adam that she had nothing to do with that story in the first place.

She brushed the thought aside. She had bigger fish to fry right now. Digging through her purse, she pulled out a notebook and pen. Then she smiled. "So what all can you tell me about this, Regina? I promise to keep this anonymous."

Regina smiled, and then leaned in closer. "Anything to screw him over. Are you ready for all of this?"

Joy flipped to a blank page. "Oh, I've been ready. Let's go."

CHAPTER SEVENTEEN

With October's arrival came the most important part of the year for River's Bend: harvest time. Adam had watched the grapes ripen into juicy, purple berries these two months. With the leaves changing to umber and scarlet, the grapes were ready to be picked.

He walked among the rows of the vines, watching workers pluck the grapes by hand and tossing them into baskets and bins. Adam had a feeling they'd finish within a week, when normally it took twice as long, if not three times. He knew the harvest would be meager this year, with the excessive rain that had destroyed so many fragile buds in the spring. Bending down, he rifled through a basket, and he sighed when he saw how many of the grapes were unsuitable for winemaking.

Adam already knew the projections, already knew how many grapes it took to make a bottle of wine, already knew that he'd be lucky to make it another year. He knew all of that, but he kept hoping against hope that they'd pull through.

They had to. Because now the vineyard was all he had.

After Joy's betrayal and subsequent departure, Adam had tried to drink his woes away, but when that had failed, he'd delved even deeper into running River's Bend. It became his obsession, his only way to make things right. That didn't mean he didn't think of Joy what felt like every other moment, or dreamed of her, or wondered how she was. If she'd gotten back with Jeremy. If she felt guilty about what she'd done.

Adam gritted his teeth. He couldn't keep thinking about that story. He'd known from the beginning that journalists were not to be trusted, and his own instincts had proven right, hadn't they? He wasn't happy about it, but it was over. The town had mostly moved on, and Adam had to move on, too.

"How are things going?" Jaime walked up to Adam, nodding and saying hello to the workers as he passed them.

Adam glanced overhead at a hawk circling in the sky. "About as well as expected."

"So, not great."

"No, not great." Lowering his voice, he added, "I'm not sure we'll make it another year."

Jaime swore, his hands in his pockets. He'd been as dedicated to River's Bend as Adam, and had turned its restaurant into a five-star culinary experience when once it had been a dowdy café. Adam didn't know where Jaime would go if River's Bend closed—would he stay in Heron's Landing? Or would he find a job somewhere else? He hated to imagine his friend leaving, but he also couldn't hope he'd stay in a place with no prospects, either.

"You don't think adding weddings and events will help?" Jaime asked.

"It'll help, but I don't think it'll be enough. We're too far in the red. If I'd started doing events a year ago, maybe..." Adam shrugged. He looked out over the acres of land, took in the vines and the grapes and the workers and the smell of the earth and the warmth of the sun above, and he couldn't imagine not doing this anymore. "We'll still host Sadie and Robert's wedding, of course. Maybe have one or two more before the New Year. But unless we get a client who has a million-dollar wedding? Doubtful."

"You know, when you first hired me," Jaime began. Then he laughed a little. "When you first hired me, I thought I'd stay here a year, tops. The last place I wanted to be was in some Podunk town in the middle of nowhere. But I ended up falling for this town, this vineyard. Now I can't imagine being anywhere else." He looked at Adam, and then he slapped him on the shoulder. "Don't give up hope yet, man."

"I'm glad you stayed," was all Adam said in reply.

The two looked out on the harvest, saying nothing, but already knowing what the other was thinking. Adam had done a lot of stupid things, but at least becoming friends with Jaime Martínez hadn't been one of them.

Like falling in love with Joy, right? his mind asked. Yes, falling in love with a woman who'd use him for money. That had been stupid. And yet...at times he couldn't be sorry for loving her, either. She'd brought him out of a dark place, with her laughter and smile. And he chose to believe that she'd loved him, in her own way.

What they'd had had been real, until Joy had chosen to ruin it.

When Adam arrived home later that evening, heart-sore and exhausted, he popped open a bottle of beer and tried to watch a game, but he couldn't concentrate. He drank another beer. A few hours later, someone knocked on his door.

Opening it, he raised his eyebrows seeing his sister on his front step. "What are you doing here?" he asked.

Grace rolled her eyes. "I'm not even sure. But can I come in?"

Adam opened the door wider. "Be my guest."

His sister had barely spoken to him since the Joy debacle, choosing to side with Joy and telling Adam he was the stupidest man alive. He knew she and Joy still talked, and although he wished his sister could see his side of things, he hoped Joy didn't try to hurt Grace like she'd hurt him.

"I'm not staying long," Grace said, "but I have to say something to you."

He raised his eyebrows. "Should I sit down?"

"You're already sitting. No, I'm here to tell you that you're an idiot, and I have no idea what Joy saw in you in the first place."

He tipped back his beer. He wished he were drunk.

"Nothing to say?" She put her hands on her hips, her freckles standing out as she frowned at him. "You're just going to sit there and look at me?"

"Did you want me to say anything?"

She made a frustrated noise. "Why can't you realize that Joy had nothing to do with that story? That it was her ex that did it? How can you not know how much she loved—still loves!—you?"

"All evidence points to the contrary. Besides, people who love you can do terrible things to you, in case you were unaware."

"Don't be condescending." Grace advanced on him and poked him in the shoulder. "You know what your problem is?"

He really, really didn't want a lecture from his little sister right now. He batted her hand away from his shoulder. "No, but you'll tell me anyway, right?"

"You're too scared to be with Joy. Too scared that it'll end like it did with Carolyn, so you'd rather find some proof that she screwed you over rather than face how you really feel. I know you love her. I see how you look whenever anyone mentions her name."

Adam gritted his teeth. If only they were kids, he could pull his sister's hair and tell her to be quiet. Instead, he said quietly, "I don't need your armchair psychological evaluation, Grace."

"Maybe not, but I'm tired of this. Don't you want to be happy?"

When he looked up, he saw tears shimmer in Grace's eyes. He was torn between pushing her out the door and embracing her. So he stayed put, and drank his beer, and tried to ignore what she'd told him.

Silence filled the room. Adam heard a car drive by, but otherwise, nothing. Only stillness.

"Can you go?" he murmured. "I'm tired."

Grace looked like she was going to say something else, but she glanced away. She bit her lip. Then she threw her arms around his neck and hugged him; it was awkward, since she was standing and he was sitting. But he patted her arm all the same as she said, "I just want you to be happy."

"I will be. Now, go. It's late." He kissed her cheek.

Grace glanced back at him one last time before she shut the front door.

FAMILY DINNERS HAD GOTTEN AWKWARD, to say the least, since the story broke. Carl had been furious, wanting to sue Joy for slander and drain her of every penny. Julia had wisely told him that they couldn't sue someone for slander if what they'd said was true, and that it would technically be for libel, anyway. Carl had muttered under his breath, and proceeded to talk to Adam about it far longer than Adam had wanted.

Now that the storm had mostly passed, family dinners were somewhat normal again. Adam, though, had a difficult time listening to the same conversation over and over again. Grace was also rather morose, and it made the rest of the family less cheery, too. Carl grumbled about the squash and wondered why they had to have chicken *again*, while Julia tried her hardest to cheer everyone up.

"I heard from Gavin today," Julia said, smiling a brittle smile. She served Adam a heaping pile of roasted butternut squash, which he ate mostly to keep his mom from being unhappy. Adam knew that Gavin's marriage hadn't been doing well, but with the vineyard and everything, he'd barely spoken to his brother in ages.

He winced inwardly. He was a selfish jerk, that was for sure.

"Gavin says that he and Emma may move back here to Heron's Landing. Isn't that exciting?" Julia unfolded her napkin in neat movements. "Then the whole family will be together."

Grace frowned. "Aren't you forgetting someone? Last time I checked, Gavin was still married to Teagan. Is she not coming with him? Or is that over and done with?"

"Hush, Grace," Julia said. Carl harrumphed. "They aren't… over. But they're taking a break. Teagan has some issues she needs to work on, that's all."

Adam knew that was code for Teagan had had another nervous breakdown and was probably in a psych ward of some hospital. After Gavin had gotten married, he and Teagan had moved to the east coast, thus removing his family from the day-to-day struggles of their marriage.

Teagan was a kind, lovely woman, but she also suffered from bipolar disorder. After her first suicide attempt, she'd been placed in inpatient care, and she'd seemed to improve. But she also disliked the medication needed to keep her moods stable. After she'd stopped taking her medication, the unfortunate cycle had begun again.

"How is Emma?" Adam asked quietly. Teagan and Gavin's daughter Emma was only seven. He couldn't imagine how she felt about her mom coming and going like this.

"How do you think she is?" Carl barked. "Her mom's a loony and refuses to do anything about it. Poor kid will never have a normal life."

"Dad," Grace hissed.

"That's enough, Carl," Julia said. "There's no reason to call Teagan names. She's sick. She can't make good decisions right now."

Carl snorted, but he didn't say anything else. The idea that a mental illness couldn't be cured with willpower didn't sit with Carl Danvers, and the family had long ago given up trying to convince him otherwise.

"Emma's starting second grade, isn't she?" Grace asked.

"That's right. Gavin thought coming to Heron's Landing would be a nice change of pace for him and Emma. Emma's had a hard time making friends, so he thought maybe the school here would be a bitter fit." Julia took a bite of her chicken, chewing thoughtfully. "She was always a quiet little thing. I think she's so shy that other children aren't sure how to talk to her."

Adam asked when Gavin and Emma would be arriving, but Julia wasn't sure. It wasn't finalized, and what with Teagan still in in-patient care, they might not leave at all.

Adam wasn't sure Gavin leaving his wife, his house, his job —everything—would help him with his demons. But, then again, he didn't have room to talk. He'd lost the woman he'd loved because she'd sold him out.

After the story broke, Gavin had texted Adam, asking him how he was holding up. Adam's reply had been brief, and the conversation hadn't gone further than that. The two brothers had been close when they'd been younger, but after Gavin had moved away and everything had happened—Teagan's health, Carolyn's death—they'd drifted apart.

Adam hoped he could get to know his brother again, if he did come to Heron's Landing. And he'd like to get to know his niece, who he'd seen only a handful of times. He may not have Joy in his life, but he was still lucky to have his family around him.

As Adam was getting ready to leave, Julia came up to him. "How are you, dear?" she asked in her quiet way.

"Fine. Just working, as always."

"I know you've been unhappy lately. But you know you can always talk to me, right? I am your mother."

Adam smiled a little. He hugged his mom and said into her neatly coiled hair, "I know, Mom. See you later."

BY THE END OF OCTOBER, with the grapes harvested, Adam sat down on the ground of River's Bend and looked out at the sunset.

The most recent financial projections had been grim: either they shut down River's Bend entirely, or find a buyer and sell it. If they were lucky, they'd sell it and break even. More than likely? They'd sell it at a loss.

The numbers floated through Adam's mind. They were sticky, like cobwebs, and he couldn't stop thinking of them. He couldn't stop thinking about Chris's face, and Leah's, and Kerry's. He couldn't get Jaime's silent, grim expression out of his mind.

But most odd of all? He couldn't get Joy out of his mind. No matter how hard he tried, she wouldn't leave.

His phone vibrated in his pocket. He ignored it. It vibrated again, and again. He fished it out, and glanced at a text from Grace. *Read this*, it said. Adam snorted. The last time he'd read something everything had come crashing down around him.

But curiosity killed the cat, and he opened the link. And to his astonishment, it was a retraction from the magazine about Carolyn, citing that they'd used an unverifiable source and that they apologized for the error. And the author? None other than Jeremy Evans.

It was the next text from Grace, though, with another link, that made him glad he was sitting down. He opened the website, and he saw an article written by none other than Joy McGuire. *Heron's Landing and its fields of grapes: a little patch of paradise in the Midwest*, the headline said. Adam's heart pounded. She'd gone ahead and published her story anyway?

But his initial anxiety slowly melted away as he read. It began with Joy moving to Heron's Landing, and her experience of moving from Chicago to a small town. The story then expanded into a glowing review of River's Bend, of its restaurant, and included a paragraph about it hosting events, as well. It was the last paragraph, though, that sent his mind into a tailspin:

I never expected to fall for a vineyard, Joy wrote, *and certainly not for the tiny town attached to it. Now that I've returned to Chicago, I've realized something: those months in Heron's Landing were the happiest of my entire life. Thanks in part to the peace found in a place like Heron's Landing, and in the happiness I experienced with the owner of River's Bend. Let's not be coy, shall we? I fell in love with the vineyard's owner as much as I fell in love with the vineyard and town itself. I hope—if I can hope for anything—that he knows that.*

Adam couldn't breathe. He couldn't take in both stories at once, and he could barely comprehend what was on his small phone screen. He knew Joy had loved him, but that she would write and publish an article saying as much? And the retraction—that must have been her doing as well.

He'd been wrong. One-hundred-percent, completely, stupidly wrong. He'd pushed Joy away the second he'd been given a reason, and he'd refused to see what had been right in front of him. He'd known he'd loved her, but he hadn't realized that that knowledge had scared him so much he'd destroyed what they'd had and then blamed Joy for that destruction.

She didn't write that article. She didn't do it. He put his head in his hands, his head whirling. *She didn't do it. She didn't do it!*

Relief, pure and exhilarating, filled him. He'd agonized so

much over her betrayal that the realization that she was inno-cent lifted a huge weight off his shoulders. His business was failing, and his vineyard was falling apart, but the woman he loved hadn't betrayed him.

She didn't do it.

He stood up. He paced. He mumbled under his breath. He thought of ways he could get her back, and then shook his head. How could he ever make it up to her? How could he convince her that he'd screwed up and that he was so sorry for it? Could she forgive him?

He wasn't sure if he could forgive himself.

He drove back home, his mind in pieces. Entering the house, he flipped on a single light and looked at the photos of him and Carolyn on the wall. He picked up the nearest one and said quietly, "She didn't do it. And I love her. I do, Caro."

Of course there was no response, but Adam felt better all the same. He'd always love Carolyn, but she was gone. She'd never return. And he knew that she'd want him to be happy.

An hour later, he got a text: *Do you get it now?* Grace asked him.

His hands were trembling as he replied, *Yes, I get it now.*

CHAPTER EIGHTEEN

A few weeks earlier...

"These are your options: either you write a retraction and I don't rat you out to the entire industry, or I rat you out to the entire industry and you lose face with pretty much any writer under the sun."

Joy watched as Jeremy scowled, his handsome face turning into something ugly and, she had to admit, a little comical. After she'd met with Regina, Joy had gathered as much information as she could regarding Regina's allegation against Jeremy, including proof of plagiarism and various conversations with other writers who had it out for him for scalping their stories. But the plagiarism was the biggest card she had. He hadn't full-on copied anyone, just a few sentences here and there. It had been subtle, and she wasn't surprised he'd gotten away with it for so long. She just hoped Jeremy took it seriously enough that he'd do what she wanted.

"And what's your proof?" he finally asked, raising an eyebrow.

Joy shoved a file toward him. He opened it with a scoff, but when he glanced at the contents, the color slowly drained from his face. "What do you want?" he asked quietly.

"I told you: I want you to write a retraction for the story about Carolyn Danvers under your name. The entire town of Heron's Landing thinks I was the one who wrote it, since you so nicely decided to use a pseudonym." At his look, she sucked in a breath. "That was your intention, wasn't it? To get a quick buck and hopefully screw me over, too?"

Jeremy shrugged. "You weren't listening to what I wanted, so I thought it was a way to make things even. Level the playing field. And what does it say about these people that they accepted it was you without any issue?" He smiled, his teeth gleaming white in the low light of the café they sat in. "Does that also include that man you were with—Adam?"

Joy bit the inside of her cheek. She shoved the folder of evidence back into her purse, saying in a tense voice, "It doesn't matter. All that matters is that you write that retraction. I'm serious, Jeremy. I will rip you to shreds if you don't do this. I might do it anyway, because you're a selfish little prick who I wish I'd never met in the first place."

"You don't mean that, Jo-Jo." He reached out to touch her, but she pulled away. "What we had was good, right? We had some fun times together. I know we did."

She agreed, but those times were over. They'd been destroyed by selfishness and a petty need for revenge, and when the times got tough, Jeremy had decided to dismantle everything they'd built together. It hurt, but at the same time, there was something freeing about realizing that.

"Look, I'm not here to talk about the past. Are you going to write the retraction or not?"

Jeremy stared at her, and then he tapped his chin thoughtfully. "You weren't like this before, you know. What changed? You aren't the Joy I knew."

Adam changed me, she thought. Falling in love with the man she was meant to be with changed her. Losing the man she loved changed her. "I'm not the girl you met when we were just out of college, that's all."

"He must've done a number on you. Adam. Because you know that if you threaten me like this, I can have you blackballed from the industry. I have enough connections who will support me regardless of your allegations." Jeremy sat back in his chair and folded his hands into a steeple.

Anxiety filled Joy, but she knew that even if she lost out on clients and couldn't work as a writer anymore, she was doing the right thing. For Adam, for Heron's Landing, for Carolyn. "Are you seriously threatening me when you're the one who's been caught red-handed?"

"I never bluff."

"No, I guess not. But my point still stands: write the retraction, or face the consequences. Your choice."

He sighed and rolled his eyes. "Fine, fine. I'll write it. When do you want it up?"

"This weekend."

"Fine."

Jeremy then asked, his voice surprisingly tentative, "How's Regina?"

"Better, now that she's moved on from you." Joy took some satisfaction in seeing him wince. Regina had been depressed, too thin, and defeated, but now she was going to therapy once a week and had gained some self-confidence back, she was a changed woman. Joy didn't know if they could ever be as close as they were, but they could at least call themselves sort-of friends as opposed to enemies. And really, the snake here wasn't Regina—it was Jeremy. He'd drained Regina dry and left her in the gutter without a look back.

"Well, I guess I should be glad she's doing well. Last time I saw her, she looked terrible."

"No thanks to you."

Jeremy rubbed his chin. "I know you think I'm this villain who's ruining people's lives, but Regina made her choice to be with me. And that town of yours made the choice to believe what they wanted. I merely facilitated those things. So if you should be blaming anyone, it's not me."

"Maybe," Joy replied. "But facilitating those things is just as bad, don't you think? Knowing that what you're going to do is going to hurt others. And I'd argue that intending to hurt is almost a worse sin."

She gazed at her ex-fiancé, wondering if there was a glimmer of humanity underneath all of that bravado. Maybe she saw it, in the twitch of his eye, but maybe it was a trick of the light. She wondered, once again, how she'd missed the obvious for so many years. But she knew it wasn't so much that she'd missed the obvious: it was that Jeremy had transformed from a somewhat shallow boy to a vicious man. He'd evolved. And with that evolution came the realization that she no longer wanted anything to do with him.

Joy stood up. She didn't feel excited by this victory: instead, she felt tired and hollow. As she turned, though, Jeremy added, "Just remember: I can ruin you, Jo-Jo. I know you think your feelings for this guy are important, but are they important enough to destroy your career? You want to live in your car because some guy said he loved you?"

She didn't turn, but instead stared straight ahead, gazing into the café. She saw couples chatting, and families sitting together. She saw a life she could've had, maybe, if things had gone differently.

Then she replied quietly, "He is that important to me. Which is something you'll never understand."

WHEN GRACE CALLED Joy a week later, Joy didn't think anything of it. She and Grace had been in contact since she'd left Heron's Landing, and Joy let the call go to voicemail. But Grace called again, and again, and finally Joy picked up the fourth time she called, thinking that something terrible had happened.

"Oh good, you picked up! I'm sorry for calling so late, but I just found out that Adam is selling River's Bend."

Joy sat up straight. Already in bed, she was typing at her computer, but she shoved the laptop off of her. "What do you mean he's selling?"

"Just that. The harvest was so bad that he feels like there's nothing else he can do. But I think he's doing it to punish himself. Joy, he read the retraction and your story. I know he did. He's been a zombie all week. He knows he screwed up."

Joy's heart squeezed, and she closed her eyes. *He read them*, she thought. *He knows I didn't write that story. And he knows I'm still in love with him.* When she'd decided to publish the piece about Heron's Landing and the vineyard, she'd almost chickened out. Part of her was still angry with Adam for refusing to recognize her innocence, while the other part just missed him and wanted everything like it was. She wanted him to realize he fucked up and that they were meant to be together.

Now, though, she had a feeling that wasn't going to happen. He wasn't supposed to sell the vineyard, the thing that mattered most to him outside of the people in his life. It signaled that he felt defeated, and that there was no going back.

"He can't sell River's Bend. What will he do? Where will he go?" Joy asked.

"I don't know. It's been in our family for generations. Joy, I know you don't owe us or him anything. He hurt you. But I also think you're the only one who can talk sense into him." Grace took a deep breath. "Will you talk to him? I promise this is the last favor I'll ever ask of you."

Joy slumped down onto her pillows. "I don't know, Grace. I don't know if that would be a good idea."

"I get it. But think about it, okay?"

"Okay. Talk to you later."

Joy did think about it: she thought about it all night, not sleeping a wink. She thought about it in the morning, while she ate breakfast and took a shower. She thought about it when she tried to get some writing done. She thought about it until her head hurt and her heart hurt.

He can't sell the vineyard. He can't. He is the vineyard.

"I have to go back," she murmured to herself the following day. "If not for him, then for Grace." She told herself she was doing it for her friend: not for the town, who turned its back on her; and not for Adam, who refused to believe her when she spoke the truth.

She may still long for him, and wish things had been

different, but she wouldn't beg for him to take her back, either. She deserved better than that.

Buying her plane ticket, she packed her things, and hoped she wasn't making a huge mistake.

WHEN JOY ARRIVED in Heron's Landing, seeing how the town looked with the changing leaves of autumn, her heart swelled to bursting. She'd missed the place, even if it hadn't treated her well in the end. It was a weird emotion, a mixture of peace at coming back and agitation that everyone still hated her.

When she drove up to River's Bend, though, her heart just about burst from her chest when she saw Adam's truck parked out front. She got out of her car and shaded her eyes. No one was in the fields; Grace had told her that they'd finished harvesting already. Looking at the building, Joy swallowed. She could do this. She could do this for Grace—couldn't she?

But she didn't even step inside. Instead, she watched as Adam himself came outside, and at first he didn't see her. Her traitorous heart leapt, and she forced herself to be calm. He hadn't apologized, had he? She'd do well to remember that.

"Joy?" he asked, his eyes widening. "What are you doing here?"

She shrugged as he came up to her, stopping within a few feet. The distance seemed gigantic, though, and Joy had never felt as far away from him as she did right then.

"Surprise," she replied lamely. "I'm not even sure why I'm here, to be honest."

"How have you been? Chicago? Grace said you were still writing."

"Yep, as always. Not much else to do these days." Joy's voice trailed away as she took him in: he looked tired, and thin, and downtrodden. He looked like he'd been run over by a tractor, if she were honest.

He rubbed the back of his neck. Then his eyes bored into her as he said, "I saw the retraction. I wanted to thank you for it. I'm sure you were the one behind it. How did you do it?"

"Oh, some threats here, and a little blackmail there. The usual. I wasn't going to let Jeremy get away with doing something like that, you know."

Adam nodded. He stuffed his hands into his pockets. His voice low, he said, "I'm sorry, Joy. I'm so sorry for thinking those things of you. I can't make it up to you, I know that. But I am sorrier than you'll ever know."

The chill encasing her heart thawed slightly. She stepped closer to him. "You thinking that I'd betray you like that—you don't know how much that hurt me." Her voice suddenly became choked with tears, and for once, she let them fall without trying to hide them. "I thought that at least you would believe me."

He looked like he was going to reach for her but then thought better of it. "I know. Grace told me that I did it to protect myself. That I found an excuse to push you away because I was falling in love again, and I'd already lost love, you know? It's not an excuse, but it makes sense." He smiled sadly. "My little sister, the armchair shrink."

"She is rather astute for her age," Joy said, feeling the tears drip off of her chin.

"And what you said to me, about waiting for the ax to fall? You were right, about everything." Adam reached out and caught a tear on his finger.

Joy closed her eyes.

"I read your story, too, you know," he said. "And I've wanted to tell you: I love you. You're everything I've ever wanted, Joy McGuire. I don't deserve you, and I don't expect you to take me back, but…" He reached into his back pocket, pulling out his wallet and handing her a small bundle of papers. "I wrote you something in return. No one would publish it because I'm an awful writer, but I wanted you to know." He brushed a tear from her cheek, so tenderly that Joy's heart was about to burst.

"I love you. You are the mermaid who showed me that dreams can come true."

She laughed, and then she cried harder. She then took the papers and smoothed one out. She could barely make out the words, but the words caused even more tears: *Joy McGuire broke my heart. She broke my heart in the best possible way, and rebuilt it again because I was broken. You see, I'd lost my wife in a tragic accident, and I'd pushed people away. Joy brought me out into the light again.*

Joy brought me joy. She is my joy. And I wanted her to know, that I love her—no matter what happens.

Joy sobbed, and now she tried to wipe the tears away. "But what about the vineyard? Grace says you're selling it?"

"She's right. It's falling apart, and it can't be salvaged. Better to sell it now than let it deteriorate." He said the words in a clipped voice, but Joy could hear the anguish there.

"It's your life, though. How can you give it up?"

He smiled sadly. "Is it my life? I'd poured so much into it, and look what I got out of it. A failing business and the woman I love hating me. I can't…it can't go on like this." He stepped close enough to take her hands: gently, linking their fingers together, the papers he'd given her crinkling between them. "I've failed it. The vineyard. I accept that. Time to take that failure on the chin and face facts."

Joy searched his face, and she realized that Grace had been right: he thought he didn't deserve the vineyard. And not only that, but perhaps he thought giving it up meant some kind of penance for hurting her.

Oh Adam. You foolish, loving, ridiculous man.

Tossing the papers into the wind, Joy threw her arms around his neck and hugged him close. He stiffened, but soon embraced her so tightly she couldn't breathe. But she didn't care. She buried her nose in the crook of his shoulder and cried until her body shook.

"I love you, Adam," she said over and over again. "I love you."

"How can you? After everything I've done." He muttered the words into her hair, touching her back, her shoulder, as if he couldn't get close enough to her. "I don't deserve you."

"We both messed up. Well, you messed up more, but…" Adam laughed a little. She said into his neck, "I was terrified of loving you, you know. I'd already gotten hurt. I should've fought for you. But when you said it was over, I didn't. I just… left. Because that's what I do: I run." Pulling away, she gazed up at him, tears streaming from her eyes. "But I'm not going to run anymore."

He took a deep breath. Then he leaned forward and touched his forehead to hers. "Thank God," he muttered.

Then he kissed her.

It was a kiss of homecoming. It was a kiss that bespoke everything that happened and everything that would happen. It represented the future, and it helped wash away the past. Joy cried, and she felt wetness on Adam's cheeks too, and she kissed him so hard they had to gasp for breath before kissing again.

"I love you, I love you," he kept saying against her mouth. He kissed her neck, fingers sifting through her hair. "Don't ever leave me again, Joy. I couldn't take it. You'll stay, won't you?"

She nodded. "Yes, I'll stay. But only if you promise me one thing."

"Anything."

"You won't sell River's Bend. At least, not until we can figure something out. If selling ends up being in everyone's best interest, then we'll talk. But don't sell simply because you think you don't deserve what you have."

Adam shuddered a little. He kissed her forehead. "I don't deserve *you*, you know."

"I know. Does anyone?" She laughed at his expression, but then she sobered. "I won't act like what you did, what you said, didn't hurt. It did. It hurts to think about it. But I think… I know that I love you enough that it doesn't hurt as much. Does that make sense?"

He hugged her close, and she wrapped her arms around him. She'd thought the safest place she could ever be would be within Adam's embrace—and she'd been right.

"Yes, it makes sense," he replied. "You make me want to be a better man, Joy. A man who doesn't run away. A man who does everything to right the wrongs he's done."

She sighed against his shoulder, feeling the autumn breeze brush against the bare skin of her neck. She inhaled the scent of leaves, and of harvest, and of Adam. She felt the warmth of his arms and the strength there, as well.

And as she closed her eyes, all she could think was: *I'm home. I'm finally home.*

EPILOGUE

Joy couldn't help but smile as she sat outside at Sadie and Robert's wedding reception a week before Thanksgiving. After the ceremony, which had been held overlooking the river at the vineyard, the wedding party had walked a few yards to the reception. A large tent had been set up across the green, and the fall leaves provided a fairy-tale like backdrop. Luckily, it wasn't too cold despite it being November.

Initially, Joy hadn't been sure she even wanted to attend Sadie's wedding, given what had happened at Trudy's. But Sadie herself had come to Joy's place to apologize and invite her personally. That had been the general tenor of Joy's return to Heron's Landing: lots of apologies, even more meals sent as apologies, and a true attempt by the locals to get back on her good side.

It felt good, she had to admit, to have people realize they were wrong about her after all. Especially Adam. She smiled wider. He'd worked especially hard to show how sorry he was.

"What are you smiling about?" Adam sat down next to her at one of the reception's tables, kissing her cheek. "Do I want to know?"

"Probably not. Although it's a shame that I wasn't consulted about the wedding party's color scheme. Turquoise and canary yellow? Yikes."

"This is Heron's Landing. We like our colors bright and garish."

She laughed. "And why is everyone barefoot? Is that a new trend in weddings that I missed?"

Adam looked at her. "Does it really matter?" he finally asked.

Wrong question. "Of course it does! I get not wanting to kill your feet in heels, but barefoot, and outside?" She made a face. "Oh well. The dresses are pretty."

"I'm sure Sadie appreciates that you approve of the dresses."

Joy couldn't help laughing. She couldn't help laughing all the time now, if she were honest. Adam did that to her, and being in a place she could finally call home. Seeing people she cared about and having them be a part of her life. It was a revelation, really. She thought she'd had that with Regina and Jeremy, but she knew now that that couldn't compare to what she had in Heron's Landing.

A slow ballad came on, and the couples on the dance floor began swaying back and forth. Twinkly lights had been hung overhead, giving the tent a magical kind of glow. Joy picked up her glass of wine and gazed at Adam over the rim.

"Are you looking at me because there's something on my face, or because you want to dance?" he asked, trying not to smile.

"Try one option and find out."

He stood, offering out his hand. "Joy McGuire," he said in a low voice, "will you do me the honor of this dance?"

"Yes, I will."

She took his hand, and he led her into the group of swaying people. She wrapped her arms around his neck, his hands on her lower back, and they gazed at each other as they moved slowly across the makeshift dance floor. The ballad was some '90s pop ballad that Joy hadn't heard in years, and she mouthed the lyrics as they danced. Adam laughed, dipping her backward. But she kept lip-syncing.

"Did I tell you that you look beautiful tonight?" He brushed a thumb across her lower back.

Wearing a dark blue, strapless dress, her bright hair in a French twist, Joy rather thought she looked like Audrey Hepburn. A delicate pearl necklace was her only jewelry; and unlike the wedding party, she wore strappy heels in a pink champagne color.

"You did tell me that, but thank you all the same." Leaning closer to him, she added softly, "You'll like what I'm wearing underneath it even more."

Adam just groaned. "Can we get out of here now or would that be rude?" he muttered.

"Very rude. You'll just have to wait."

In revenge, he pinched her ass, and she burst out laughing.

When the dancing returned to the usual wedding kind of dances, Adam pulled Joy off the dance floor and out of the tent, taking her to a bench not far from the recently harvested vines. Ever since Joy had returned, she and Adam had worked tirelessly to book events at River's Bend using Joy's contacts in Chicago for assistance. They weren't absolutely sure they wouldn't have to sell the place, but things looked much better than they had initially.

The moon bright and shining, Joy pulled her shawl closer around her. It was finally that time of year when it got cold at night. Seeing her shiver, Adam wrapped an arm around her; she snuggled into his side.

They sat like that for a while, simply gazing out into the horizon, the moon slowly moving across the sky. They heard owls hooting, and the sounds of laughter and conversation from the tent behind them. Adam rubbed her arm.

"Joy," he said. "I wanted to ask you something."

Being pressed up against Adam like this had made Joy sleepy. She stifled a yawn to reply, "What?"

He shook her a little. "Don't fall asleep on me yet."

"I'm soooooo tired. I feel like I was the one who got married, but I didn't. You better be quick, otherwise I'm liable to miss everything you say."

He tipped her face up toward him. She could just make out his expression in the moonlight. "Then I'll be quick."

To her utter astonishment, he moved down off the bench and went down on one knee in front of her. At first her brain couldn't compute what he was doing—she was rather tired—but then she gasped like a ninny. "Adam!" she blurted.

"Joy McGuire, love of my life, woman of my dreams, writer extraordinaire: will you marry me? I don't deserve you, but that doesn't mean I won't try to get you to be mine anyway."

Joy's sleepiness disappeared completely. She sat up straight, staring at him, and her heart pounded so fast she felt a little dizzy. She clutched at the bench. "Are you sure?" she whispered.

He laughed a little, uncertainty in his voice. "Of course I'm sure." He rifled through his pockets and pulled out a ring box; Joy could see the ring sparkle in the low light. "I bought this, didn't I?"

"Adam. Oh my God." And then to her surprise and his, she slid down onto the ground and threw her arms around him. He toppled backward. "Yes, did I say yes? I can't remember if I said yes. Yes, I'll marry you!"

"Thank God." Adam wrapped his arms around her and kissed her. She laughed as he kissed her, and then he set her back on the bench and took her hand. "I hope it fits, and that you like it. I used another ring of yours for the size."

"So that's where my silver ring ran off to."

"Mmmhmm." He slipped the band onto her left ring finger. She held it up to the light, and her heart pounded even harder.

"I love you," he added.

She stared at the diamond, and she couldn't wait to see it in full light. Then, in a saucy voice, she replied, "For this rock? I love you, too."

When Adam laughed, Joy knew that they only had the best things ahead of them.

GRACE GLANCED at herself in the mirror inside the bathroom of River's Bend, and she took a deep breath. *You can do this. You can do this.* She touched up her lipstick one more time. She made sure she didn't have anything in her teeth. Then she forced herself to leave and do what she came here to do.

It was Sadie and Robert's wedding, of course, and Grace had come for that, and to support her brother at his first event at the vineyard. But she'd also made the decision to stop looking at Jaime Martínez from afar and actually make a move. Joy's happiness with her brother had given her enough of a reason to at least try. It was worth a shot, wasn't it?

Of course, Jaime could say no. He could say she was just Adam's little sister and go back to her parents. He was seven years older than her. Fear congealed in her stomach, and she almost chickened out. If he said no, she couldn't avoid him in a place as small as Heron's Landing.

Walking outside, she looked at the moon, and took another deep breath. *You can do this. You can do this.*

Grace wore her nicest dress, a dark green dress with a boat-neck that showed off the curve of her neck and shoulders. It was modest, but sexy in a way as well. The green set off her eyes, and her hair was braided into a complicated crown. Joy had helped her with her makeup, and if she didn't look pretty, she at least looked grown up.

You're not a little girl anymore, she chastised herself. *You're twenty-three years old. An adult. Start acting like it.*

Grace entered the tent where Jaime had been sitting, but she didn't see him. Had he already left? Her heart sank. She'd been looking at herself in the mirror so long that she'd missed her chance. She wanted to sink down onto the ground and cry out in frustration.

Then she heard his voice. "How did you like the trout? Aha, I thought you'd enjoy it. I knew I could convert you." She turned her head, and she saw Jaime doing what he did best: talk about his food. She smiled. He'd cooked all of the food served at the wedding, and it had been a hit, to say the least.

Grace knew Jaime could work anywhere in the world. He was an extremely talented chef. So why stay in little Heron's

Landing and work at a place like River's Bend? She didn't understand it, but she didn't want him to leave, either.

She watched as he moved about the tables, chatting and laughing. His dark hair had grown out lately, and he looked rather rakish. His dark eyes gleaming and looking handsome in his suit, Jaime had been the center of Grace's dreams for so long she couldn't remember a time when she hadn't been in love with him. When he'd arrived in town five years ago, little Grace Danvers had looked on his handsome face and her adoration for Jaime had been cemented.

Everyone seemed to know of her feelings for him—except Jaime.

She watched as he exited the tent, and she left by a side entrance. She followed him, some yards behind, wondering where he was going. When she realized he was going to a secluded patch not far from the vineyard's main building, her heart leapt. This was her chance.

Grace froze, her feet not moving. *I can't do this*, she thought. *I can't. I can't.*

Yes, you can. You can do it.

She didn't know where she gathered her courage, but before she knew it, she was standing in front of Jaime with her heart in her throat. When he saw her, he looked...relieved?

"Oh, Grace, it's you. What are you doing out here?" He'd been leaning against the wall of the building, his hands in his suit pockets.

Grace fiddled with her corsage, which had scratched her wrist. "I wanted to talk to you."

Jaime finally looked at her. "What? Did you say something?"

Raising her voice, she said, "I wanted to talk to you?"

"Oh, okay. What's up? Is your brother annoying you again?"

She stepped closer. She could make out the small cleft in his chin, how he had stubble already, how there was a smattering of silver in his beard. He was only thirty, but she found the silver attractive. It made him seem distinguished.

She fiddled with her corsage, twisting it around.

"You look like you're going to be sick. Do you want to sit down?" Jaime glanced around, but there was only grass to sit on. "Let's go find a bench."

"No, I don't need a bench," she blurted. He looked at her. "I mean, I don't need to sit down. I'm all right."

He didn't seem convinced. "What did you want to talk to me about?"

"I wanted..." Grace came closer. She forced her hands behind her back so she wouldn't keep messing with her corsage. "I wanted to tell you..." The words stuck in her throat, like a thorn, and she couldn't speak.

"Wanted to tell me what?" He peered at her, his eyebrows furrowed.

Just say it. Say it. Say it.

SAY IT!

"I like you!" She blurted the words, almost shouting them into the darkness. At his blank look, she blushed so furiously she probably looked like a tomato. "I mean, I find you attractive and have for some time."

He didn't say anything. Then he laughed—laughed! Grace's face burned so hotly now she was surely on fire.

"Grace, you're sweet. You are. But you're my boss's little sister. You know we couldn't ever be a thing, right?" His voice was kind, conciliatory, like an older brother would to soothe a younger sibling.

It was, in a word, humiliating.

Tears sprang to her eyes. That was it, then, she thought glumly. He thought of her as a little sister, and not as a grown woman. She glanced down at her dress, and it suddenly seemed girlish and silly.

"Oh geez, Grace, I'm sorry. I'm not good at this." Jaime stepped toward her, but didn't touch her. "Please know that I care about you very much. But not like that. Thank you, though, for telling me." He smiled a little and then chucked her on the chin. "You'll find someone—I know you will. It just won't be me."

Grace almost stumbled, she wanted to run as fast as she could. She wanted to hide under a rock and never face the light of day again. But as she was about to leave, she looked at Jaime one last time. And her heart lurched.

A courage she hadn't known she possessed filled her. The words she said next were calm, assertive. "I'm not a little girl, Jaime Martínez."

His eyes widened a little.

She stepped closer. And then closer. "I'm not a little girl. I'm not your kid sister. I'm a woman. I might be younger than you, but this isn't some silly infatuation. I wouldn't have told you otherwise." She stepped so close that only inches were between them. She breathed deeply, and she saw Jaime's nostrils flare.

"I know you're not, but that doesn't mean I'm the man for you." He sighed and murmured, "I'm sorry."

And before she could react, he walked away into the night.

ABOUT THE AUTHOR

A coffee addict and cat lover, Iris Morland writes sexy and funny contemporary romances. If she's not reading or writing, she enjoys binging on Netflix shows and cooking something delicious.

irismorland.com